Kage Baker

Or Else
My Lady Keeps
the Key

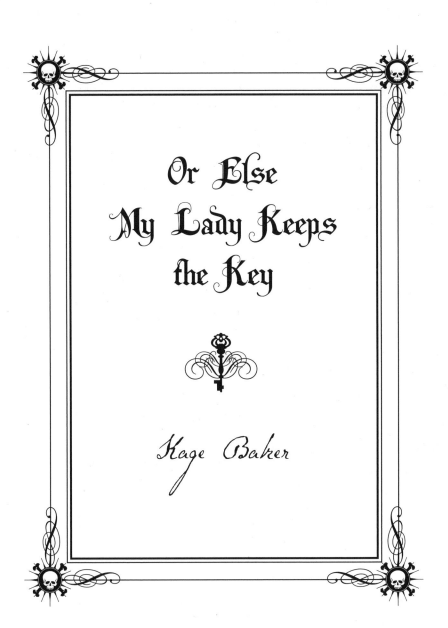

Or Else My Lady Keeps the Key

Kage Baker

SUBTERRANEAN PRESS 2008

First Edition

ISBN
978-1-59606-162-0

Subterranean Press
PO Box 190106
Burton, MI 48519

www.subterraneanpress.com

*Fondly dedicated to
Mike Rettinhouse
Teacher. Scholar. Pirate.*

ONE:

The Letter

ON THE 16TH DAY of April, 1671, a man walked down Tower Street in old Port Royal and came to the Bluebell Inn. He stood in the street a while, looking up at the hanging sign. The daubed blue flowers were unmistakable, and in any case he could read the name perfectly well, having had some education. Still, he hesitated to step inside.

His name was John. To some people he was known as John James. He had been a London bricklayer's apprentice who killed a man and was sent to the West Indies as a consequence. He had been several things since then: redleg bond slave, runaway, pirate, and most lately patriotic gentleman of fortune, for he had just returned from doing his bit sacking Panama with Captain Henry Morgan.

This very morning he had gone ashore, bidding farewell to his late commander. Morgan had returned his salute with a gloomy wave, and headed straight for the nearest tavern for a stiff drink before reporting to Governor Modyford.

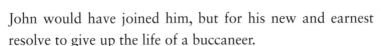

John would have joined him, but for his new and earnest resolve to give up the life of a buccaneer.

It wasn't that the Panama expedition had been short on glory and adventure. It was that, when all had been honestly measured out afterward, John's share of the loot amounted to a mere fifty pounds; and this had decided him to turn his hand to bricklaying once more.

Moreover John had seen madness and nightmares walking in the noonday sun, and left good comrades dead in the ashes of the old Spanish city. Still, there was a responsibility to discharge before he might begin his new life.

He squinted up at the sign again. He reached inside his coat, fingered a bit of paper hidden there, and sighed. At last he squared his broad shoulders and went into the Bluebell.

When his eyes had adjusted from the sea-glare to the dimness of the common room, he saw that the Bluebell was a clean place, as taverns in Port Royal went. No whores on the prowl, at this hour of the day, and no drunks asprawl at the tables. Only a sound and smell of onions frying in the kitchen, pungent, and a landlord who emerged from a back room and looked at him expectantly.

"What d'you lack, sir?" the landlord asked him. Taking a step nearer, he sized John up and grinned. "You've come back with our Admiral from Panama, ain't you? Then welcome, sir! What you want is rum, my bully."

"Thank'ee, no," said John, narrowing his eyes. He was young, and big, and strong as an ox, with a broad simple face; but he wasn't that green. "I carry news for a lady. Have you got a Mrs. Waverly staying here?"

The landlord's expression changed, became unreadable. "We have. May I tell her your name, sir?"

"She won't know it," said John. "But it's John James. You can tell her I've brought her a letter from Panama, and a private word if she'll hear me."

The landlord ducked his head in acknowledgement and walked into the back. John heard him climbing a staircase. John looked around again, shifting his weight from foot to foot. The floor of the common room was plaster laid down over planking, rapidly crumbling away to chalky punk in Port Royal's climate. John made a note to come back, once he'd set himself up in business, and offer to put in good herringbone brick paving at a reasonable rate.

He looked up and saw that the landlord had reappeared silently, like a ghost. "Madam says please step upstairs, sir," said the landlord. "First chamber on the left."

John followed him as far as the stairs, and climbed alone. He came to the top of the stairs, meaning to knock, but the door to the first chamber on the left was wide open. A lady stood within, staring at him. Her face was deadly pale, so white John thought she might be going to faint. Her gray eyes were fixed on him; her red mouth was set and tight. She clenched a handkerchief in one hand.

"Ma'am," John said, and bowed awkwardly.

"You must be from Tom," she said. She had a sweet voice. Her accent was refined. She'd been Sir Thomas Blackstone's mistress, so John supposed she'd been at court. He wondered uneasily if she was going to scream, or faint, when she heard his news. He cleared his throat and brought out the letter, with its daub of candle wax sealed by a thumbprint.

"I'm sorry to say, ma'am—" he said.

"Oh, he's dead. He's dead. Is that what you've come to tell me?"

"Yes, ma'am. He said to tell you, he died singing."

She jerked as though he'd shot her, but her face twisted into a smile, a horrible thing to behold. "Did he?" she said. "Pray excuse me a moment." She turned on her heel, smart as a soldier, and marched to a chair. There she sat, covering her face with her hands, and wept, wracking sobs wrenched up dry from the roots of her heart.

John fidgeted, turning the letter in his big square hands. He saw again Tom Blackstone lying on the pallet in the makeshift hospital in Panama, red-faced and sweating. Before the fever had risen, Blackstone had called for pen and paper, and written out the letter in his fine hand. He'd sealed it and handed it to John.

"She won't be expecting the print of my ring," he'd told John. "She pawned it herself, long since. But do give her the letter, won't you? Mrs. Clarissa Waverly, at the Bluebell. You can remember that, can't you? And do tell her I died singing."

John had been enough of a tender-hearted booby to shed a tear and cry, "Oh, courage! You won't die!" Blackstone had given him a pitying look and called for wine. Two hours later he'd rattled out his last breath.

Too vividly John remembered the stink of Blackstone's bandages in the close foul air of the room, and the way Blackstone's voice had broken as he'd crowed out the old song:

> *The serving men doe sit and whine, and*
> *thinke it long ere dinner time:*
> *The Butler's still out of the way, or else*
> *my Lady keeps the key,*
> *The poor old cook, in the larder doth*
> *look, where is no goodnesse to be found*

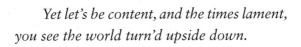

Yet let's be content, and the times lament,
you see the world turn'd upside down.

Now his lady, having wept for him, sighed and wiped her face with her handkerchief. Some of her paint came off on it. She blew her nose, sat straight and looked up at John. John proffered Blackstone's letter.

"From him, ma'am."

Her mouth crumpled a bit at the edges, but she took the letter and broke the seal. She read swiftly, her gaze darting back and forth along the lines. At last she folded the letter closed, and tucked it into her sleeve. She regarded John thoughtfully.

"He said you were in his confidence, concerning his mission for Prince Rupert."

"I was, ma'am."

"Have you brought Prince Maurice from Panama, then?"

John reddened. "As to that, ma'am...we did find the lost prince. Got him without paying out any ransom money, neither. But he'd been a long time in a Spanish dungeon and he wasn't, er—"

"Tom said he'd gone mad."

"In a manner of speaking, ma'am, aye," said John, remembering Prince Maurice's gray moon face and blank dead eyes. He wondered whether Mistress Waverly had ever heard of *zombis*, and decided not to go into details.

"We reckoned Prince Rupert might be happier, not knowing what become of his brother after all, see. And then Tom went and died and I had errands to run for the Admiral, and I couldn't watch the prince, and some fellows let him out and...well, he's been lost again, ma'am. I'm sorry for it, but that's how it is."

"Then it was a fool's errand," said Mrs. Waverly. "And farewell my sweet Tom. However…" She was silent a moment in thought. At last she rose, giving John a brave smile. "Good man, I owe you a great deal. Pray step below and call for a bowl of punch, and we'll drink to Tom. Then you may hear something to your advantage."

John obeyed readily. He was fairly sure she wasn't the sort to make him dead drunk and rob him after he'd passed out, like Hairy Mary who worked the waterfront over by the Turtle Crawl.

When he came back up Mrs. Waverly had smoothed her hair and refreshed her paint a little. She showed him to a chair and pulled another close, sitting nearly knee-to-knee with him. She encouraged him to speak of himself, of brave Admiral Morgan and the thrilling battles John had seen at Chagres Castle and Panama.

Her interest in these matters lasted until the landlord brought up the punchbowl, and took his leave after ladling out the first two cups for them. John thought the man gave him an ironical smile as he left. But the punch smelled all right, and John resolved not to take a second cup in any case.

"To Tom Blackstone," he said, lifting his cup. "A rare brave comrade. And a clever fellow."

"To Tom Blackstone," said Mrs. Waverly, her voice catching on a little sob. "Oh, what a clever fellow he was." She drank deep and set her cup aside. "Well. My dear Mr. James, you have been such a good friend to Tom, and so kind to me; I wonder whether I might further impose on your good nature?"

"Well, er, ma'am," said John, "I'm sure I'd be happy to perform any service you might require." It occurred to him that she might construe lewd meaning in what he'd just said, and he winced. Yet his baser instincts woke and sat bolt upright, in hopeful surmise.

"I knew you would say so," said Mrs. Waverly, smiling into his eyes. "I will be frank with you, Mr. James. You know there was a ransom demanded for Prince Maurice's safe return."

"Four thousand pounds, aye," said John.

"We collected it in London, when Prince Rupert engaged our services. We brought it with us to Barbados, to treat with a certain Spaniard there, who claimed to know where Prince Maurice was being held. He merely directed us to meet another Spaniard here. We began to suspect that we were being led in a fools' dance. Therefore Tom took the money, gold in sealed bags, and hid it secure, lest we should fall amongst thieves in our search.

"As it fell out, we have no brother to send home to the prince," and here Mrs. Waverly's voice slowed, and she twisted a lock of her hair about her finger. "And I have lost a dear friend, and you have lost a valiant comrade-at-arms. Tom being dead, how shall Prince Rupert hear what became of the four thousand pounds? For all he may know, Tom paid the ransom in good faith and was treacherously slain by Spaniards. I think we are owed the money, you and I, for our pains."

John blinked at her. He got the full import of what she was proposing, but her use of *you and I* set his heart pounding.

"Four thousand pounds," he repeated, attempting to sound keen.

"Let us divide it, dear Mr. James," said Mrs. Waverly. "Two thousand each."

"Seems fair," said John, trying not to dribble his punch. He wondered what unlikely thing might happen next. Heavenly angels flying in through the window, bearing plum duff and sausages? Closely followed, perhaps, by Father Christmas?

"I knew you would say so," said Mrs. Waverly. "We have only to find the money."

"Don't you know where it is?" John sat straight, as the pink clouds dissipated somewhat.

"In a general way," said Mrs. Waverly, with a graceful wave of her hand. "We bespoke our rooms here and then Tom left with the money. I thought he'd taken it to meet his contact. I didn't see him again until a fortnight later, when he returned in a fine temper and told me he'd hid the money, but missed the man and would now be obliged to chase after him, perhaps as far as Chagres. We quarreled. I regret it now…Oh, to think I shall never see him again!"

She drooped, tears in her eyes. John was moved to take her hands in his.

"Aw, ma'am, it makes no odds. His last thought was of you, wasn't it? And him being so particular about sending you the letter and all."

Mrs. Waverly squeezed his hands. "But he was my rock, my brave steadfast hero, a very bulwark to a poor frail woman! Where shall I find another such? Shall I rely upon you?"

She leaned close and John had an excellent view down the cleft of her bosom. "Be sure you may, ma'am," he said, breathless.

"What a dear soul, what a kind soul you are, Mr. James! Did you see the letter, before Tom sealed it?"

"No, ma'am."

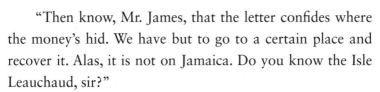

"Then know, Mr. James, that the letter confides where the money's hid. We have but to go to a certain place and recover it. Alas, it is not on Jamaica. Do you know the Isle Leauchaud, sir?"

"Leauchaud? Ay," said John. "Not hard to get to, at any rate."

"Then I will leave it to you to make the travel arrangements, as I am sure you know a great deal more about these things than I do," said Mrs. Waverly. "But I must beg you to pay for our passage, for in truth I have scarcely any money left."

A tear trickled from her eye as she said it. John's heart contracted. But his purse contracted too; he had calculated that his fifty pounds would just about set him up in business with a brickyard and proper tools of his own. He put the thought down as ungentlemanly, and considered too what he might do with two thousand pounds.

"I'll see to it," he said. "Never fear."

TWO:

They Embark

JOHN WENT DOWN TO one of the wharves and found a ship, the *Fyrey Pentacost*, bound for Barbados with a cargo of tortoiseshell and logwood. The captain was agreeable to taking on supercargo at a price, since Leauchaud was one of his ports of call, and since he had already agreed to take another traveler on board. Smiling, he quoted John a price for the passage. John winced but said "Done," thinking of his share.

Early next morning he called for Mrs. Waverly at the Bluebell, and found her waiting with her packed trunk. All the same, they were like to have missed the boat; for it fell out that there were certain sums owed to the landlord that needed paying, and Mrs. Waverly's purse was not equal to the debt. John paid.

"That was very kind of you," said Mrs. Waverly, as they stepped into the street at last. "But you mustn't pay for the hire of a porter to carry our trunks. I believe I can just scrape together sixpence—"

"No need," said John, a trifle brusquely, and swung her trunk up on his shoulder. He tucked his own sea chest under his other arm. Mrs. Waverly looked at him, wide-eyed.

"Oh, sir! Indeed you are a Hercules for strength!"

John was a little mollified at that, but he merely said. "Strong enough, ma'am," and strode off in the direction of the wharf. She followed him. They went crunching through drifts of broken shells, winding their way between the street vendors and avoiding all the unpleasant things folk had thrown into the street overnight.

Emerging onto the waterfront, they faced the brilliant glare of a hazy morning. The plaster walls of the houses reflected the dazzle back on the salt mist coming off the sea, or was it steam? John felt sweat prickling under his shirt, and squinted up at the sails being unfurled on the *Fyrey Pentacost*. They hung limp as curtains in a parlor.

The crew were getting ready to cast off. The first mate greeted John with a black scowl as he came aboard. He bit back whatever remark he had been about to make, though, when he beheld Mrs. Waverly gracefully lifting her skirts as she stepped up the gangplank. Men fell over themselves to offer her helping hands down into the waist.

"I thank you very kindly," said she, smiling at them all. "Will some good gentleman show us to our cabins?"

"This way, ma'am," said the first mate, bowing and gesturing aft. "And sir," he added over his shoulder to John, in a peremptory sort of way.

Cargo had been pushed back hastily on the under-deck and bulkheads hammered into place to form three cabins, windowless and low. Mrs. Waverly regarded them in dismay, but made no complaint as John set her trunk down inside. She merely opened her trunk and set about making up a bed in the sort of box that had been provided. John set down his sea chest and peered at the tiny space allotted him. He grunted, dug out his hammock, and strung it up instead.

As he was tying it off, there came a double rap at the cabin door. John opened it, ducked down to see who had knocked, and found himself face to face with a sullen-looking black servant.

"Captain Sharp's compliments, and requests the pleasure of your company at table this evening," the servant recited, in a bored sort of way. He had an oddly flat, nasal accent.

"Oh. Right," said John. The servant did not stay for further pleasantries, but stepped away sidelong.

John heard the same double rap, the same formula recited, and Mrs. Waverly's clear reply: "Please convey my delighted acceptance to the captain and assure him I will be prompt. At what o'clock are we to dine?"

"Half past seven, ma'am."

"Thank you."

The same sidestep, knock and recitation, and then a new voice responding: "Oh! Why—well—that's exceedingly decent of Captain Sharp! Yes, indeed. I'll be there. Yes. Thank him, please."

It was a male voice, an educated one. It sounded middle-aged.

They had to put out boats with sweeps to row the *Fyrey Pentacost* out of the harbor; they were obliged to keep the oars dipping until they were nearly to Port Morant. At last a breeze freshened and the sails flapped, then bellied as they caught the breeze in earnest.

John was leaning on the rail, feeling pleased that he wasn't one of the poor devils rowing away in the boats, when Mrs. Waverly came up from below, parasol over her shoulder. She put her hand on his arm.

"Dear Mr. James, perhaps we might have a word," she said in a low voice. "I am a little concerned for my good name."

"Have some of these bastards been treating you improper?" asked John, and felt his face grow hot. "Hoping you'll pardon my plain talk."

"Oh, no, no indeed. But there have been inquiries made as to our relations, you see."

John stared at her a moment, wondering why anyone would be asking after his old mother and ten brothers and sisters in Hackney, before he got the sense of what she'd said. His ego sat up and preened a bit. "Well, it's nobody's business—"

"Exactly, but now and again one does encounter a puritanical sort of ship's master who assumes the worst about one," said Mrs. Waverly, coloring a little. "So I have given out that I'm a new-made widow, and you are my late husband's manservant."

John's ego fell, wounded. "Servant?"

"Oh, I know it cannot be to your liking, dear Mr. James; but it will help us avoid scandal, and in any case it's only until we reach Leauchaud," said Mrs. Waverly. "Tom and I had to devise such shifts many a time, as we traveled. Why, on one occasion I was obliged to disguise myself as a boy!"

It was a diverting image. John contemplated it a moment before swallowing hard and muttering, "Well, but things stood a certain way between you and Tom Blackstone."

"That's true. Yet I do count you as a friend, Mr. James; and who knows whether we mightn't become very dear friends indeed?" Mrs. Waverly looked into his eyes. "Please, my dear, go along with the disguise this once, as a favor to me?"

"Well," said John. He looked down at her, in her gown of yellow cotton sprigged with forget-me-nots. "Ain't they going to wonder why you aren't in black?"

Her lip trembled. "I hadn't the money to buy a mourning gown," she said. So then John felt like a cur dog, and said of course he'd go along with the game.

So John went before Mrs. Waverly to the great cabin that evening, and cleared his throat and announced her, as he supposed a servant ought to do. Four pairs of eyes watched his performance, and hers as she entered. Besides Captain Sharp and the first mate, Mr. Harris, there was the black servant who had conveyed the dinner invitation; also a little mild-looking man of about fifty, wearing thread-loop spectacles, who was introduced as Mr. Tudeley.

"Mr. Tudeley is on his way to Barbados," explained Captain Sharp, as he held out his wineglass. The black servant filled it. "A new position, I take it, sir?"

"I hope so, indeed," said Mr. Tudeley. "My sister and brother-in-law keep a pie-house there, you see, quite a profitable one. They have intimated they require a clerk, and were so good as to send for me after Squire Darrow's plantation failed, I being then at loose ends."

"Why, sir, I hope a pie-house is steadier work than a plantation!" said Captain Sharp, with a wink at the others.

"I, too. There wasn't any fault in my accounts," said Mr. Tudeley, looking miserable, for he had caught the wink. "No fault of mine at all. But Mr. Cox, that was the manager, Mr. Cox had taken to drink, and neglected the place shamefully. I said so at the time. The indentures were insolent and lazy, too. What could I have done?"

"I am sure you did your best," said Captain Sharp. "And may I introduce the Widow Waverly? And Mr. James. Her man."

Mr. Harris looked knowing at that, and the black servant stared in a fairly open way. John scowled, but Mrs. Waverly smiled.

"He was simply devoted to my poor husband, you know, and a better factotum I could not hope for," she said, with a graceful wave.

"Thank you, ma'am," said John.

"And we are taking you out to Leauchaud, as I understand?" said the Captain to Mrs. Waverly.

"Indeed, sir."

"You'll be taking the waters for your health, I dare say?"

"No; I have certain matters to resolve, concerning my husband's inheritance," said Mrs. Waverly.

"Oh, well! You ought to try the waters, while you're there," said Captain Sharp. "I've been, and it did me a world of good. You would think you were in Bath! Mr. Shillitoe's had handsome pools built for invalids, and a pump room beside."

"How charming!' said Mrs. Waverly. "Perhaps I shall call on Mr. Shillitoe."

"Now, is it Mr. Shillitoe runs the place, or Mr. Leauchaud?" inquired Mr. Tudeley, leaning aside as the black

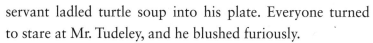

servant ladled turtle soup into his plate. Everyone turned to stare at Mr. Tudeley, and he blushed furiously.

"Chah! The name comes from *L'eau chaud,* hot water," explained the black servant, with a snort of amusement. Now it was Captain Sharp who turned crimson.

"How dare you address my guests! Hold your tongue, damn you!"

There was a moment of uncomfortable silence, in which the servant met Captain Sharp's glare with a smoldering look of his own.

"So it is French, then!" said Mrs. Waverly, with a bright little laugh. "Of course. No doubt some Frenchman or other discovered it. Well, well. What a pleasant thought."

"And I'll have none of your insolent looks," Captain Sharp continued to the servant, "or you'll earn yourself a flogging. Now, fetch out the sherry." The servant hooded his eyes and bowed stiffly. He withdrew from the cabin.

"I declare I took no offense, sir," protested Mr. Tudeley. "I wouldn't have the poor slave beaten on my account."

"He isn't a slave," said Mr. Harris. "He's a damned freedman who gives himself airs."

"Freedman or no, he'll find himself cutting cane in the sun one of these days," said Captain Sharp, with an unpleasant smile. "Fetch a good price too, I don't doubt. Well! Let it alone. May I offer you a slice of the smoked pork, ma'am?"

The conversation touched on the price of sugar next, followed by the weather and local gossip. John was largely excluded from the conversation. At first he was relieved, not having much of a knack for genteel chitchat, until it occurred to him that he was being spoken around because he had been introduced as a mere servant. Then he felt a bit resentful.

He was spooning up the last of his soup when he heard a liquid sound on the other side of the bulkhead. The sound suggested certain distinct images; he felt an answering twinge in his bladder. A moment later the servant returned with a decanter of amber liquid, and set it at Captain Sharp's elbow, with a narrow-eyed smile.

"Your sherry, sir," he said.

"Ah. A glass with you, gentlemen?" said Captain Sharp.

"I thank you, no," said Mr. Tudeley. "Not after the claret. I have a poor head for strong drink."

Captain Sharp regarded him in amused contempt. "As you like," he said. "You, my man?" he inquired of John.

John peered at the servant, wary. The servant raised his eyebrows. He gave a barely perceptible shake of his head.

"Er," said John. "Thank you. No."

"You, Harris?"

"Please," said Harris, with his mouth full.

"Sherry for Mr. Harris and myself, Sejanus," said Captain Sharp.

"Certainly, sir," said the servant smoothly, and filled their glasses. "Shall I clear away the soup tureen, sir?"

THREE:

Old Friends

THEY MADE LITTLE HEADWAY next day, for the wind swung around and the *Fyrey Pentacost* labored in the swell with a seesawing motion that sent Mr. Tudeley below, green as turtle soup. His groans drove Mrs. Waverly from her cabin, in turn, and she went above-decks for a stroll. *Strolling* proved impossible, though a sort or lurching progress from handhold to handhold could be managed. Several helpful crewmen put themselves in her way to catch her lest she fall against them, which she did. After the second time her hat was blown into the rigging, though, she made her way across the rocking deck to John's side, where he stood at the rail. She clasped his arm to steady herself.

"Shall we get there soon, do you think?"

"Two or three days, I reckon," said John. "At this rate."

"Dear God," said Mrs. Waverly. John looked at her sidelong.

"I been thinking about that money, ma'am."

"I, too, I assure you."

"I been reckoning it up. Four thousand pounds in gold, in sealed bags—that'd be a great heavy sum to be carrying, wouldn't it? In sovereigns, anyhow. Tom couldn't have lifted four thousand sovereigns by himself, let alone carried it off on his own to hide it. I reckon the only way he could have done it was if it was in five-guinea pieces. That'd amount to eight hundred of 'em."

"I suppose it would, yes." Mrs. Waverly gave him a slightly hostile glance. "You're rather good at sums, I must say."

"It's only like reckoning up how many bricks go in a course, ma'am," said John. "So. Allowing it was in five-guinea pieces, allowing it was eight hundred, and reckoning the weight at five stone and some—that's still a powerful lot for one man to carry about. And I was just wondering, ma'am, how Tom lugged it off to Leauchaud without anyone noticing and robbing him. You're sure he had it, are you?"

"Of course I am," said Mrs. Waverly. "Don't be silly. I must have searched the room a dozen times while he was gone. And it *was* in five-guinea pieces, thank you, in sealed bags in an ironbound chest, quite a small one, considering. I saw it. And in any case, I have his letter! He tells me plain where it's hid."

"Is there a map in the letter? Might I have a look at it?"

"Oh, Mr. James!" Mrs. Waverly put her hand on her heart. "How can you ask such a thing? Tom's letter contains remarks of a most private and passionate nature, and I am sure he never meant any eyes but mine own to read it. Spare a lady's blushes, do!"

"All right. Meant no offense, ma'am." John hung his head and glared down at the white water hissing past the

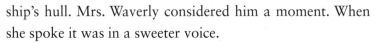

ship's hull. Mrs. Waverly considered him a moment. When she spoke it was in a sweeter voice.

"I would that Tom had trusted me, as he seems to have trusted you," she said, and sighed, and leaned against John. "I loved him to distraction, and yet he held a part of himself aloof from me, always. But you are not like that, are you? I sense you have a kind and honest heart. If he had told you anything that might give a poor woman advantage now, you would surely tell her."

"Be sure I would, ma'am," said John, powerfully conscious of the warmth of her against his side. "But he never told *me* anything about the money. Only that it was hid safe."

The ship dropped into the trough of a wave, smacking them with salt spray, and its lurch sent Mrs. Waverly tottering backward. John put out his hand and grabbed her lest she fall. He pulled her close, wrapping an arm around her. She looked up into his eyes. Her lips parted, and she sort of melted against him. "Oh, thank you," she said.

John inhaled her breath, which was sweet with caraway because she'd been chewing comfits against seasickness. He wondered if they might get down into the cable tiers, where there was a chance to do it in a certain amount of privacy; he wondered if she was the sort of woman to be put off by the sight of a few rats running about. All this in the hushed moment in which she half-lay on his arm, gazing up wide-eyed. Then there was a voice close by his ear.

"Excuse me, lady." Sejanus stepped around them and leaned over to empty the captain's chamber pot to leeward.

"Do you mind?" snapped Mrs. Waverly. She gripped the rail and stood straight.

"I was just keeping her from falling," said John. "On account of the rough sea."

"Oh, yes," said Sejanus, in a neutral voice. "Very rough today, indeed." He lowered a bucket on a rope to pull up some rinsing-water. As he straightened up he looked aft at the horizon, and frowned. "We're being followed," he said.

John turned to look. There was a ship coming along, well over the horizon, keeping in the *Fyrey Pentacost's* wake to starboard. She was a low thing, no bigger than a schooner, and the fact that her fore-and-aft sails were all patched and stained with many colors had made her harder to see. But John saw well enough the men crowded on her deck, and the glint of their weapons. As he watched, the craft sped nearer.

"Bugger," he said. He knew well enough what they were, having cruised in just such a vessel himself. "Pirates astern!" he bawled.

"Oh God!" murmured Mrs. Waverly, and ran below. As John's cry was echoed by the tardy lookout and men ran to the rail to see, Sejanus placidly rinsed out the captain's chamber pot.

All was confusion for a few minutes, with Mr. Harris shouting orders until the captain ran up on deck. The helmsman swung the tiller, and the *Fyrey Pentacost's* square sails luffed as she changed course and turned to run before the wind, like an agitated hen. The pirates merely cut straight across her wake and made for her port side, close enough now for John to make out their grinning faces.

"Blow them to Hell!" screamed Captain Sharp. "Mr. Partridge, serve out the muskets! Load the gun!"

Two of the crew got busy with the ship's little rail-mounted one-pounder, and soon got off a shot that fell short of the mark; the pirates hooted and came on, their craft skimming over the water fast and light. By the time the gun was reloaded and aimed again, the pirates were close enough to nail the gunner with a musket ball between his eyes. He fell with the slow match in his hand.

John, seeing the firefight commence in earnest, ducked down and went below. He wasn't a coward, but he had a good head for odds and nothing much worth stealing, and he didn't feel like dying that day. He made his way to his cabin in the dark, and there loaded the pistol he'd brought with him, largely by touch.

"Mr. James?" Mrs. Waverly's voice came from the other side of the bulkhead. She sounded tense, but not as though she was crying. "What ought we to do, Mr. James?"

"Stay out of the way," said John.

"Are we in danger, Mr. James?"

"Might be," said John. "Depends on how angry the captain makes 'em. I've got a pistol, and I won't let 'em hurt you."

Mrs. Waverly said nothing for a moment, in which time they heard the musket fire die down and the sounds of scuffling overhead, followed by the ringing of blades. "You are very good, sir," said Mrs. Waverly at last.

"What was that?" Mr. Tudeley's weak voice floated from his cabin. "What's toward? Is that fighting? Good God!"

"Pirates," said John, stepping out of his cabin. He leaned against Mrs. Waverly's door, watching the dark passageway steadily.

"Oh Jesus Christ!" groaned Mr. Tudeley, and there was a crash suggesting he had fallen to his knees. "Oh, dear Lord deliver us! Lord, Lord, what have I ever done to deserve Thy wrath?"

"Take heart," said John. "The captain might beat 'em away."

It didn't sound as though that was much of a possibility now, however. John heard a lot more thumping overhead, and Captain Sharp yelling furiously. "Cowards! You damned cowards! *Shoot him!* Sejanus! My pistols—"

Then there was a terrific crash and a last thump. The noise of the swords stopped. John heard Mr. Tudeley weeping, and men muttering, and quick footsteps to and fro overheard. He heard someone coming down the companionway. At the far end of the passage, shadows blocked the light as men milled around, poking into the bales and boxes there.

John took a deep breath, and a firm grip on his pistol. He had no idea what he'd do with his one shot. He wondered whether Mrs. Waverly was the sort of woman who'd rather die than be raped. If she turned out to prefer death, he could blow her brains out, he supposed; otherwise the pistol would be pretty useless.

Footsteps were coming along the passage. Someone was carrying a lamp. John watched the yellow flare approaching, and saw gradually the glint of light on peering eyes and teeth. A dirty bearded face. A man wearing only rawhide breeches, holding a cutlass low and his lamp high.

John let his breath out.

"Sam Anslow, ain't it?"

"Who's that?" The man halted, lifted his lamp higher.

"It's me, shipmate!" John put all the cordiality he could muster into his voice, and stepped forward. "John James. I was at Panama with you. Sailed under Bradley."

"God damn," said Anslow, and grinned. "I remember you! You was on burial detail at Chagres Castle."

John felt drunk with relief. "So I was. Just lately come home with the Admiral. You weren't in the fleet?"

"Not I," said Anslow. "I reckoned I'd take my chances in Tortuga. A man has to earn his bread."

"That's true," said John.

"How much did you make out of it?"

"Fifty pounds."

"That was my share, too. Lousy business, weren't it?"

"Fortunes of war, and all."

"So," said Anslow. There was an awkward pause. "Here you are."

"Aye," said John. He had what seemed a brilliant flash of inspiration. "I went home and straightaway married. The wife and I was on our honeymoon."

"Oh! Congratulations," said Anslow, hanging the lamp on a nail and offering his bloody hand to shake John's. "So you weren't working this cruise?"

"For a lubber like Captain Sharp? Not likely!" John chuckled, as convincingly as he could. "Now, I hope there ain't going to be unpleasantness between us and your lads, shipmate, eh? What with me being a new bridegroom and all. I got my bride's feelings to think of."

"Oh, right," said Anslow, and glanced uneasily over his shoulder. "That's for Captain Reynald to say, of course. But it'll be all right. I'll vouch for you." For the first time he seemed to notice the cabin behind John. "The missus in there?"

"Aye."

"Congratulations on your wedding, ma'am," said Anslow in a raised voice.

"I thank you, sir," said Mrs. Waverly, through the bulkhead.

"You're kindly welcome," said Anslow. He looked sheepish. "Well. Business is business."

"So it is," said John. "Shall I go help you shift cargo?"

"You wouldn't mind?"

"It ain't *my* property," said John, shrugging.

FOUR:

The Harmony

WHEN THEY WENT ON deck at last, with Mrs. Waverly clinging tightly to John's arm, the cleaning-up had begun; which was to say, dead men from both sides were being pitched overboard, and the blood was being swilled off the decks with buckets of seawater. The survivors of the crew of the *Fyrey Pentacost* were lined up along the rail, being jeered at by the survivors of Captain Reynald's crew. Captain Sharp was slumped against the mast, clutching a lace-edged handkerchief to his eye. Captain Reynald, a lean Frenchman, was surveying his new quarterdeck and looking pleased with himself.

"Captain sir?" Anslow touched his forelock and led John and Mrs. Waverly forward. "This is my mate John, what I mentioned, and his bride."

"Madame!" Captain Reynald gaze fixed on Mrs. Waverly. "Enchanted!" He took her hand and kissed it. "Please have no fears for your safety. We are a gallant band of adventurers, and respect the honor of a woman. Mr.

Anslow informs me your husband is a comrade of his."

"How very kind," said Mrs. Waverly, with a bright artificial smile.

"And you are welcome to our crew, sir," said Captain Reynald to John, looking him up and down. "We are short-handed."

"Er," said John. "Well—"

"Hear me!" Captain Reynald turned to the prisoners. "I offer each man among you the same choice! You may go over the side with your captain, or you may take the oath to join our company and live free. Will you join us, for liberty and treasure? What of you?" He pointed his cutlass at Mr. Tudeley, who had been hauled up from his cabin sobbing and now stood swaying and white-faced, from sickness and terror both.

"Oh, Jesus, sir! I wish to live!" cried Mr. Tudeley.

"Trés bien! Welcome, friend. And you?" Captain Reynald swung the tip of his cutlass to Sejanus, who was next in line.

"I cheerfully accept your offer," said Sejanus. About this point it sank in on Mr. Tudeley that he had just joined a pirate crew, and his mouth opened for a cry of horror. Somehow, though, all that emerged was a sort of croak.

Captain Reynald moved briskly down the line, and one after another of the *Fyrey Pentacost's* crew joined up, except for the ship's cook and Mr. Harris, who had been beaten unconscious and couldn't voice a preference. He was dumped unceremoniously into the bottom of one of the boats, and lowered over the side; the ship's cook was shoved down to join him and so, after a certain amount of furious invective and threats of the rope's end, was Captain Sharp.

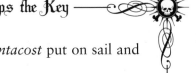

They were set adrift, as the *Fyrey Pentacost* put on sail and tacked about.

All this while John had been revolving in his mind what he ought to do, and was just clearing his throat and preparing to approach Captain Reynald when Mrs. Waverly's fingers pinched off the circulation in his arm.

"Husband, may I just speak a word in your ear?"

"To be sure, wife," said John, walking with her into the waist, where nobody much was standing at the moment.

"I must commend you on your swift thought, and your care for mine honor," said Mrs. Waverly. "Knowing full well that you will never be such a beast as to press your advantage against a helpless female. Now, my dear: on no account must we let slip, amongst such people, any least detail regarding our plans."

"I wasn't about to tell 'em," said John, indignant. "What kind of a mooncalf do you take me for?"

"I'm sure you're quite clever," said Mrs. Waverly. "Just as I am sure Mr. Anslow is a kind gentleman, and Captain Reynald too for all I know. But I think it best to be discreet amongst so many other persons of uncertain character, don't you? We will go along for the present and bear with our misfortune, trusting that we will have the opportunity to escape at some point and make our way to Leauchaud."

"Right," said John. "It's only that I was getting out of the business, as it were, and now I'm on the account again whether I will or no. Any court's going to say this was an English ship, and hang me up alongside that frog captain."

"Only if we are caught," said Mrs. Waverly. "And in any case I shall plead for mercy, and swear that you only did it to protect me."

"How likely is that to work?"

"It has never failed before," said Mrs. Waverly, smiling graciously at Captain Reynald.

The ship was rechristened the *Harmony*, and that night they found themselves invited to another dinner with the captain; only this time it was at a long trestle table set up belowdecks, in the crew's quarters.

"Welcome, friends," said Captain Reynald, who had put on a clean shirt for the occasion. "Madame." He bowed deeply and once more kissed Mrs. Waverly's hand. "I trust you will find the viands to your liking. They have been prepared with these own hands of mine."

"Really," said Mrs. Waverly, as he led her to a place at the head of the table.

"Indeed, madame. We are a happy community of brothers here; I am the leader only in matters of war and philosophy."

"Philosophy?" said John, taking his seat to Mrs. Waverly's left, since Captain Reynald had taken the seat to her right. Sejanus took a seat next to him and sat looking around, in great enjoyment; Mr. Tudeley, still pale and miserable, found himself seated far down the table.

"Indeed, my friend. We are a utopian fraternity of corsairs, rebels against the entrenched corruption of kings and merchants. We have refused the chains of Civilization and live in perfect equality here, upon the wide sea, the mother of liberty. Is it not so?"

"Yes, Captain," chorused the crew, in tones that suggested they'd heard his speech a multitude of times.

"For example: all delicacies shall be shared in common among us." Captain Reynald drew the serving platter close, and carved one of a pair of Captain Sharp's capons. "My brother corsairs share in whatever bounty we find. Will you have some of this chicken, madame?"

"I thank you, yes," said Mrs. Waverly. He loaded her plate with generous slices, to the point where the men at table looked narrowly at what was left.

"Perhaps you are surprised by such men; perhaps you expected us to be little better than savages," continued Captain Reynald.

"I confess I scarcely knew what to expect," said Mrs. Waverly.

"Though of course it is a fact that among *civilized* men, you will generally find filth, moral turpitude, decadence and lies, whereas if you make the acquaintance of primitive Man in his natural element you will find him a noble and honest creature," said Captain Reynald, with a gracious nod in the direction of Sejanus.

"I wouldn't know, sir," said Sejanus dryly. "I was born in Massachusetts."

"Pardon me," said John, a little irritated by Captain Reynald's attentions to Mrs. Waverly. "This sounds all right and proper, and I'm grateful to know we've fallen in with such a high-minded lot; but, since we're on the account, let's talk business. Have we got a commission?"

"Why, of course," said Captain Reynald. "Signed by the governor of Tortuga."

"Allows us to go after anybody but the French," said Anslow, grinning. "And even them, if the captain don't feel they're yew-topian enough."

"How do you know?"

"I regard them through the spyglass," said Captain Reynald. "If the captain is dressed in great finery and his men are ragged, clearly he is oppressing them and it is our duty to liberate the ship."

"We got the *Triomphe de Bourbon* that way," volunteered one of the crew. "There was a ship, by God!"

"Pity about that reef off Curacao," said another man, looking mournful.

"It is no matter," said Captain Reynald. "We have this fine ship now, and the *Fraternity;* we shall cruise together and increase our fleet. Others will come to join us, and who can say? Perhaps we will find a suitable island on which to set up our community, and govern ourselves democratically."

There were responses from the crew of "Oui, c'est vrai," and "Right you are," and "We're all looking forward to that day, I'm sure," none of it in tones of great enthusiasm.

"But in the meantime," Anslow said to John, "It's the old rules. No Purchase No Pay, but no damned shares to the King nor the Duke of York nor no governors, neither!"

"Not even the governor of Tortuga?"

"He is a reasonable man, and is content with a modest bribe," said Captain Reynald. "And even I, the captain, even my share is no greater than that of my fellow corsairs. We are equal in all things!"

"Really," said Sejanus.

"Indeed," said Captain Reynald, filling Mrs. Waverly's glass with Captain Sharp's best rhenish. "I propose a toast, my friends: to universal liberty and the brotherhood of all mankind!"

They drank, all of them; even Mr. Tudeley, who screwed up his face as though he was about to swallow poison. After the first taste, though, he sighed and had another.

FIVE:

Theology

THE CONGENIALITY ON BOARD lasted about as long as the delicacies plundered from Captain Sharp's private store held out. When they were back to jerked beef and rum, the mood reverted to one a bit more like what John expected on a pirate ship.

Equality or no, Captain Reynald reserved the right to order them about. The first task John and his mates were set was tearing down the poop and quarterdecks, so the *Harmony* became a flush-decked fighting platform.

"I have been meaning to ask you about something," said Sejanus, as he levered out the windows of the great cabin.

"What?" said John, catching the panes before they shattered and setting the window down flat.

"When did you and your mistress marry?"

"How dare you ask such an impertinent question, sir?" said Mr. Tudeley, sweating as he struggled to pry loose the wall-paneling by the privy closet. He set down his crowbar and pulled off his spectacles to wipe them on his sleeve. "Though to speak truth, Mr. James, I had wondered myself."

"We ain't married," said John. "It was a ruse, what d'you think? On account of I didn't know what these fellows would be inclined to do with her."

"Ah! Very gallant of you," said Mr. Tudeley.

"Just so," said Sejanus. "So...you *are* her servant, then."

"Aye," said John. He took up Mr. Tudeley's crowbar and hooked it into the paneling that had defeated Mr. Tudeley. A wrench, a grunt, and the panel popped off and bounced across the room like a playing card.

"And yet, you were a pirate before," mused Sejanus. "How does a man go from piracy to serving in a lady's chamber?"

John turned slowly, with the crowbar in his hand. "Well, ain't you too clever by half?" he said quietly. "I reckon if I was to crack your crown and pitch you out that window-hole, there ain't anybody'd know it wasn't an accident but me and Tudeley here."

"Too clever," said Sejanus, nodding, though he did not move. "Yes, that's me. And you aren't as stupid as you look, either. I'll hold my tongue."

"But..." Mr. Tudeley's face contorted as he tried to think through the relationship. "But...good God, sir, d'you mean the woman is a strumpet? You brought her aboard for *immoral purposes?*"

Sejanus burst out laughing.

"You dunce, who in hell goes to sea for a fuck?" said John crossly. "We could have laid up in an alehouse if that was all we'd wanted. Look, mate, here's the truth of it: me and her man was mates in Panama, and he died, and I come back to tell her." Hastily he laid down a new level of untruth, like paint. "Her health ain't the best, and she wanted to take the waters at Leauchaud. I was only squiring her out there on my old mate's account, as a last favor like."

"Mmm-hm." Sejanus took up a crowbar and set about dismantling the window frame.

"You must excuse me," said Mr. Tudeley. "I have moved so long amongst indecent people, I scarcely recognize an honest man when I see him anymore."

"That's all right," said John, pulling the cabin's wainscoting away.

"I have often thought it must be something in the air of this place," said Mr. Tudeley, in a mournful voice. "I used to imagine the tropics would be like Paradise, when I was in London. Reading Raleigh's book, you know, imagining green palms waving in the sunlight, and luscious fruits growing all year round, and quaint birds and monkeys. It seemed another Eden.

"I'd no idea I'd find such heat, such rogues and drunkards, such...sweat and stink and filth! Mr. Cox had been a reasonable and upright man in London; Squire Darrow had great reason to trust him with the plantation. Yet I watched him rot before mine eyes in this sweltering heat, doing no more but lying in his hammock all hours of the day and swilling rum. I spoke with him long and earnestly, pointing out his duty, and was told to go to perdition for my pains. Was that fair, sir, I ask you?"

"I don't reckon life's fair, mate," said John.

"And yet, I know I was blamed," said Mr. Tudeley. He put his spectacles back on and bent to pick up the wooden slats that John was scattering everywhere. "Mr. Cox drinking himself into an early grave, who was left to blame but me? Squire Darrow's reproach was almost more than I could bear. Yet it is all of a piece with the course of my life."

"Mm-hm," said Sejanus.

"Do tell," said John.

"Nothing but disappointments," said Mr. Tudeley. "Disappointed at school, in my marriage, in my prospects, all hopes blighted. It's enough to make a man rail at God."

"Chah!" said Sejanus. "Why don't you, then? If it makes you feel any better."

Mr. Tudeley shuddered. "Bitter as the crust of my life has been, how much worse might it be was I to call down the wrath of the Almighty?"

"Now, see, you're like my father," said Sejanus.

"How dare you!"

"There he was, lying in chains in a pool of shite, rolling to and fro as the slave-ship rolled, and what did he say? 'Oh, merciful Damballah, I don't know what I did to make you angry with me, but I'm sorry!' And then there he was, sold naked as a baby on the auction block, and dragged away to sweat on a tobacco plantation, and what did he say? 'Oh, merciful Damballah, I know I must have earned your anger, but if you'll show me what you want me to do, I'll do it!'

"And then there he was, lamed when a wagon rolled over his leg, and sold away to old Reverend Walker of Boston, who made him fetch and carry anyway and married him to an ugly woman, and what did he say? 'Oh, merciful Damballah, I just know you have a reason for all the sufferings you've inflicted on me, and maybe someday you'll please to tell me what it is?'

"And you know what he always said to me? 'Respect the loas, Bandele! They are great and powerful and they watch over us always!'"

"What's a loa?" asked John.

"Well, what can you expect of your heathen gods?" said Mr. Tudeley with a sniff. "Our Lord God Almighty is the *true* divinity."

"And so said Reverend Walker," said Sejanus. "He gave me schooling, he said to me, 'Little Sejanus, I cannot save thy father's obdurate soul, but I shall save thine.' He said, 'The Lord Almighty in His infinite mercy has visited the burden of slavery upon thy sinful people, and thou must bear it patiently, for it is part of His divine plan.' I said to myself, *Oh, yes, that'll make me love your Lord Almighty!*

"But he preached at me every day, did the Reverend Walker, trying to save my black soul. He'd lean out the window and preach at me the whole time I'd be weeding in his garden. He preached at me every mile of the way I had to carry him to and from the church, after he got too old to sit a horse.

"I said to myself, these two old men are fools. Great and powerful Damballah couldn't save his people. Great and loving-merciful God carrying on the spiteful way He does makes no sense either. So at last I resolved I wasn't believing in any of them.

"And you know what happened then, just last year?"

"What?" inquired John, pausing to mop his sweating face.

"We had moved to Virginia," said Sejanus, smiling at the memory. "They passed a law there. The news came the day after I became an atheist. 'All slaves come into the country by ship will remain slaves. All slaves born into the country to be manumitted after thirty years' service.' And I was just thirty. 'There it is,' I said To Reverend Walker, 'I was born here. I'm free!'

"He signed my manumission and he said, 'Then God has blessed you, Sejanus. Kneel with me and pray!' And my old father said "You see? The loas have set you free! Let's make them an offering in thanks.'

"I said 'Thank you, but I think I'll just get my black arse out of here before the law changes.' I took my manumission paper and I set off. Last I saw, those two old sad men stood there watching me walk away down the lane. All their holy-holies between them couldn't set me free. Only a loophole in the law, and me having the wits to jump through it."

"Oh, that's just blasphemy," said Mr. Tudeley.

"But I worked my way this far and here I am, free as a bird," said Sejanus. "How free are *you*, God-fearing man?"

"How'd you like dumping Captain Sharp's pisspot for him?" said John. Sejanus scowled at him.

"At least I got paid wages for it," he said. "And I *chose* to be here. Nobody, man or god, will ever ride my back again."

SIX:

The Santa Ysabel

JOHN WAS DEAD-TIRED WHEN he went to bed that night. He retired to the cabin, for Captain Reynald had graciously allowed him to keep it, "in order that the fair lady might enjoy her privacy". Sejanus had been granted a hammock where the rest of the crew slept, and got on famously with them, and everyone seemed to have forgotten that Mr. Tudeley had a cabin somewhere aft. Privacy for John there was none, of course; only Mrs. Waverly curled up in the narrow cot, frowning at him when he blundered in.

"Do put the candle out soon, won't you?" she said, sharpish. "I had just fallen asleep."

"Sorry, ma'am," said John. He swung himself up into the hammock and groped for the candle, pinching the flame out. He lay there, swaying in the pitch darkness, wondering uneasily what he should do if he needed to break wind.

The question occupied him to the edge of consciousness. Just as he was slipping over the edge into sleep he was jerked

back by a small sharp noise, very loud in that confined space. For a moment he lay petrified with embarrassment, thinking he had farted. As he recollected the sound, however, he realized it had been more of a metallic sound; not unlike a coin or small bauble striking the deck.

"What is it?" said Mrs. Waverly, out of the darkness. She sounded full wide awake.

"Somebody dropped something."

"I don't believe so," she said. John heard her rustling about. "I believe you were dreaming, Mr. James. I heard nothing. Do go back to sleep."

The deck was flush, all the pegs sanded down and all the nail-holes stuffed with oakum and tar. Now John saw why Reynald's men put up with his silly-arse ideas about universal brotherhood; for the captain knew his craft. He had the *Harmony* rerigged, giving her fore-and-aft sails for speed.

Reynald stalked her aft deck in satisfaction, gazing up at the spars and lines, now and then ordering an adjustment. When she was in full trim they caught a wind and ran, and made twelve knots. She might be broad in the beam, but now the *Harmony* was fast as a hare, and answered the helm like a willing bride.

No sooner was she apt for work but she found employment.

"Allons!" Captain Reynald grinned and closed up his spyglass. "Flag of Spain! Anslow, signal the *Fraternity*. We pursue!"

John, who had been cleaning the one-pound gun, looked up in interest. He could just make out the tilting pyramid of sail on the northern horizon, and the unwieldy bulk under it that suggested a merchant galleon. He cheered up considerably. Cargoes of tortoiseshell and logwood were pleasant enough to have a share in; the same went for sugar and rum. But the prospect of Spanish emeralds, or gold, or silver from the mines of Potosi, was enough to make the mouth water.

"What's happening?" said Mr. Tudeley, who had been helping him by holding the rags and bucket of grease.

"We're going into action," said John, grinning as he watched the *Fraternity* wheel about and take off after the Spaniard like a coursing greyhound. The *Harmony* came about too and cut after her, and men catcalled and ran up into the rigging for a better view as they sped along.

"Oh dear God," said Mr. Tudeley. "And now I shall be party to murder and robbery."

"No!" said John. "That's a Spanish ship, see? Now, you and me being English, our consciences are clear. They're the enemies of the nation, so for us it's a proper act of war."

"But there has been a treaty signed," said Mr. Tudeley. "We are at peace now, or hadn't you heard?"

John had heard something of the sort, but he shrugged. "Like as not they'll declare war again, when they hear what we done at Panama. And, you know, they're only Papists after all." He looked around at Captain Reynald. "Shouldn't care to be a Frenchman," he added thoughtfully, "because they're Papists too, and I don't know how they square their consciences going after Spaniards."

"I can't bear this," said Mr. Tudeley, gathering up his rags and bucket. "I'm going to my cabin."

"Just fetch up the powder and shot first, will you?" John called after him, watching avidly as the distance closed between the *Harmony* and the Spaniard.

The Spaniard was the *Santa Ysabel,* and the *Fraternity* had already engaged her to port when the *Harmony* came storming up to starboard. Little puffs of smoke were showing, here and there as muskets were fired.

John, who had been waiting impatiently for Mr. Tudeley's return, sprinted below and found him struggling upward with his arms full of shot, holding a powder horn between his teeth. "Oh, Bleeding Jesus," cried John, and grabbed him up bodily and ran back on deck with him.

"Le gouvernail!" Captain Reynald was roaring, pointing at the *Santa Ysabel's* rudder. They were within point blank range. "Shoot! Shoot her!"

"Aye sir!" John slammed down Mr. Tudeley and relieved him of a gunball. He grabbed the powder horn, loaded, turned for a bit of wadding—

"Where's the damn wadding?"

"The what?"

John spotted a book peeping from Mr. Tudeley's coat pocket. "Here." He grabbed it, tore out a page and shoved it down the gun, over Mr. Tudeley's cry of outrage. The ball was rammed down, and then—

"Where's the slow match?"

"You didn't ask for one!"

"Oh, you whoreson ninny—"

"Merde! C'est incroyable," muttered one of the musketmen, and dropped to his knees beside John, who aimed for the *Santa Ysabel's* rudder. The one-pounder was tiny, no longer than John's arm, but easy as a pistol to aim. They waited until the rise and the musketman dabbed his slow match to the touch hole. The gun fired; the little ball sped true and smashed pintle and gudgeon both, a beautiful shot if not much use. Hastily they reloaded, tearing another page from Mr. Tudeley's book ("You bastards! That's Boethius's *The Consolation of Philosophy!*" raged Mr. Tudeley) and fired again, John praying for lightning to strike twice.

He heard the shot strike home but couldn't see it; yet his luck must have held, for the *Santa Ysabel* wallowed and swung, drifting sidelong and turning her bow toward the *Fraternity*. Over the cracking of musket-fire John heard the Spanish tillerman cursing, as the *Harmony* cruised past and came around again.

Now the *Harmony* had the advantage, for her tops were full of buccaneers, crack marksmen. They picked off the one sharpshooter in the *Santa Ysabel's* main top, whose attention had been focused on the men in the *Fraternity*. His covering fire stopped as the crew of the *Fraternity* pulled close enough to grapple and board.

John leapt up and ran below, grabbing a cutlass and axe from the arms-rack. He felt the crash as they ground into the *Santa Ysabel's* side, but kept his feet and ran on deck once more, in time to see a Frenchman cut down right in front of him by a Spanish musketball. Mr. Tudeley was on his hands and knees, crawling crabwise. John kicked the dead man's cutlass toward him.

"Come on!" he roared, as he spotted the Spanish marksman re-loading on the quarterdeck of the *Santa Ysabel*. He hurled the axe, which spun end over end and took the

Spaniard full in the face. The man dropped with three inches of steel spike in his brains. John ran on and vaulted the shifting uneasy space at the rail, landing on his feet aboard the other vessel.

His enthusiasm evaporated, as it tended to do in the heat of battle, when his cold rational self woke to blood and mayhem. Panic drove him then, and so far had done well by him, enabling him to mow through his assailants.

He looked around now and promptly ducked, as one of the defenders swung a Toledo blade at him. The man had a better blade and was a better swordsman; John knew no style but a butcher's, but he was bigger and had the reach on the other, and was scared besides. His opponent fell with a grunt, cleft at the shoulder, and didn't move again. John saw men boiling up from belowdecks and yelled in terror. He put his blade up and beat away the first, and beheaded the second, and by slow degrees hacked through the crowd to the companionway and stood there gibbering, killing the Spaniards before they could come out, like a housewife smashing beetles.

Then there was blood all over the deck, all over the treads of the companionway, and John was looking down at dead men. He peered around, confused. Something was on fire, smoke tendrils were drifting up now from the hole at his feet. He saw Sejanus, grinning white through a mask of blood as he fought, and behind him another black man, one John did not recognize. The man was a near-giant, whaling away with a big squared blade; his strokes mirrored those of Sejanus, with eerie precision. It looked almost like a martial dance.

Then a grimacing enemy rose into John's field of vision, pointing a pistol full into his face. John shouted and ducked, cutting the Spaniard's legs out from under him. He rose and to his astonishment saw Mr. Tudeley, holding his cutlass out as though it was a poker, attempting to fend off an opponent. The other lunged forward and sliced away Mr. Tudeley's left ear, and cut the string that held his spectacles on his face to boot. Yet he overreached.

His stroke carried him against the rail, in which time Mr. Tudeley had time to realize what had happened. He caught his spectacles and clapped a hand to the side of his head, disbelieving; then burst into tears. He ran full tilt at his enemy and impaled him on his blade. The man fell, yanking the hilt from Mr. Tudeley's grasp as he dropped. Mr. Tudeley stood there weeping, streaming blood down his neck. He fumbled for his handkerchief and clapped it to where his ear had been, murmuring "You bastard, oh, you bastard. How shall I wear my spectacles now?"

"Victoire!" someone was shouting. John turned to stare and saw Captain Reynald swinging a bloody cutlass on high. All the Spaniards were down, dead or dying. The *Santa Ysabel* had been taken.

When they ventured below they saw they might have taken the *Santa Ysabel*, but they weren't likely to keep her. A fire had been started somewhere down in the hold, and thick white smoke was billowing up. Some of the men went down with buckets of water to try to put it out, but they couldn't find where it was before the smoke drove them out again, blinded with tears, choking.

So in the end it became a frantic game, running down with wet cloths bound over their mouths to grab what bales and boxes they could and drag them up on deck, to be swung over to the *Harmony*. John and Anslow hung off the stern on ropes and kicked in the windows of the great cabin. They got a lot of the Spanish captain's candlesticks and plate that way, as well as some armor and navigation gear.

But all the while the smoke was getting thicker, and the fire could be heard now, crackling away somewhere deep. The *Fraternity* ungrappled and cast off, sailing free just as the first red flame appeared. Little bright tongues danced up through a blackened patch of deck. "Abandon ship!" someone shouted, and John joined the general rush to scramble back on board the *Harmony*. They cast off and moved away from the *Santa Ysabel* with bare moments to spare: indeed the *Harmony's* paint was bubbled and discolored from the heat, where she'd lain too close. The same breeze that pushed them away fanned the blaze, and looking back John could see the little flames running up the *Santa Ysabel's* shrouds and lines like sailors.

They did not stay to watch it burn, but beat away north. Still it was visible a long while behind them, as night fell, an inferno pitching up and down on the black water.

SEVEN:

Tortuga

I T OCCURRED TO JOHN to wonder where Mrs. Waverly had been during the battle. He assumed she had sensibly remained in her cabin, but thought he ought to go down and ask her how she did. So, as the wounded were being laid out groaning, John took a horn lamp and went below.

"Ma'am?" he said, knocking on the door. There was no answer. He wondered if she had fainted, and opened the door and shone the lantern in. There was no sign of her.

"What are you doing, Mr. James?" He voice came from behind him. He swung around to see her approaching him from the direction of the foc'sle.

"What're *you* doing?" he demanded, in his surprise. She looked pained.

"Seeing to private matters," she said primly.

"Oh."

"I trust the engagement is over, and Captain Reynald won?"

"Aye, he did, ma'am."

"And were many poor fellows wounded, on our side?"

"We're fair cut up, ma'am, but the other side's are all dead."

"I must do my best to tend to our boys, then," said Mrs. Waverly. She shoved past him into the cabin. He heard her rummaging in her trunk. She emerged with one of her shifts, tearing it into strips, and went up on deck. John followed her.

There was a sort of Guy Fawkes' Night air on deck, with the smell of gunpowder strong and the loot from the *Santa Ysabel* piled up all untidy in the lanternlight. The wounded sat or lay here and there, while the others were eagerly opening barrels and crates to see what they'd got. Mrs. Waverly knelt at once to play the ministering angel to the hurt. John shrugged and walked forward to the plunder.

"What'd we take?"

"Commodities," said a Frenchman named Belanger, and spat. "Maize flour. Salt. Le tissu coton, what d'you call her, calico?"

"Hell," said John. "Well, the candlesticks and plate ought to be worth something, eh?"

"We will get a good price for all," Captain Reynald told them. "Turn it all into gold at la belle Tortue! Madame, truly you are a saint." He crouched beside Mrs. Waverly, who was binding up the stump of Mr. Tudeley's ear.

"It is a lady's duty, sir," she said, smiling at him. Mr. Tudeley paused in his lament long enough to watch sourly as Captain Reynald kissed Mrs. Waverly's hand, and then resumed:

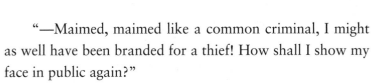

"—Maimed, maimed like a common criminal, I might as well have been branded for a thief! How shall I show my face in public again?"

"Your scar shall be a badge of honor, my friend," Captain Reynald told him, gazing into Mrs. Waverly's eyes.

"Oh, gammon and spinach," snapped Mr. Tudeley. "And what am I to do about my spectacles?"

"Tie them around the back of your head," advised Sejanus, who had come through the entire fight without a scratch. He found a bit of string and bound Mr. Tudeley's spectacles on for him, though he had to fasten them around the outside of the bandage Mrs. Waverly had bound on, the ends of which stuck up on Mr. Tudeley's head like rabbit ears. "There! Now you can see."

"Though I shan't wish to look in my shaving-glass," moaned Mr. Tudeley. "What indignity."

"Have some rum," said John absently, for he was rummaging in one of the boxes he'd salvaged from the Spanish captain's cabin. It looked to have nothing much of value in it. He pulled out a comb and a bundle of letters bound with ribbon, a block of sealing wax, a sort of jointed ivory tool containing a toothpick and other personal grooming devices. There was a smaller box inside, too. John opened it and whistled. He saw a pair of earrings, gold set with dangling emeralds, and a twist of paper that when opened contained four loose pearls of varying sizes.

"Here's something, anyway," said John, holding out the box. Captain Reynald rose and peered into it, then dipped out the earrings.

"Adornment for a beautiful woman! Let this share go to Madame, our selfless nurse!"

"Sir!" Mrs. Waverly's eyes gleamed as she beheld the gold and emeralds. "I couldn't possibly accept such a generous gift!" But her hand went out for them pretty fast anyway, and closed tight on them. John, seeing that Captain Reynald hadn't noticed the pearls, closed them up again in their paper twist and pocketed them.

There was some grumbling among the men about Mrs. Waverly getting the earrings, but Captain Reynald spoke a few more high-flown words about gallantry and beauty. In the end the wounded crawled or were carried off to the foc'sle and the unscathed lugged the plunder below, and that was that.

They made for Tortuga next day, sailing through fair weather. Only the weather was fair; there was a glum and quarrelsome mood on board the *Harmony*, and not just from resentment over Mrs. Waverly being given the emerald earrings. (Though it was true that one or two malicious parties accosted John in various corners, to tell him that they had positive proof he was being cuckolded by Captain Reynald. The horns being false, John still felt profound irritation at being suspected of wearing them.)

No, the main disquiet amongst the crew was generated when they began to complain of the loss of small valuables. One man missed a little pearl-handled knife, another a lucky trinket, still another a ring he had taken from a dead man. No one could point a finger at who might have done it.

And two of the crew got in a fight over what one had said about the other's religion, and knives were drawn, and one of them lost an eye in the fight. His screams and moaning kept the whole ship awake, until his desperate mates fed him enough rum to shut him up. Captain Reynald was aghast. He lectured both the combatants next day, long and earnestly, on the need to set aside old sectarian grudges in favor of secular unanimity.

And, in addition to his other woes, Mr. Tudeley developed a toothache that nothing could ease, though his shipmates pointed out that holding a mouthful of rum would kill the pain, or at least keep him from caring about it.

And the stores of food turned out to have been miscounted, and they had to go on half rations the last few days, though Mrs. Waverly was excepted. The captain explained that a delicate female must not be expected to endure the same hardships as a seasoned corsair.

"Next thing they'll do, they'll start talking about how a woman's bad luck on a ship," said Sejanus, winding a length of fishing-line. "You'd better mind the lady, lest they put her over the side. Nothing more dangerous than a pack of scared whites."

"Bugger off," said John, watching grumpily as Captain Reynald demonstrated the use of an astrolabe to Mrs. Waverly. "Why'nt you go over on the *Fraternity* and serve alongside the other darky, if you find us so damn funny?"

"What other darky?"

"The other one," said John. "Him that was right beside you in the thick of the fight, when we took the *Santa Ysabel*."

"I didn't see any other black men."

John stared at him. "How'd you miss him? He was big as a house. Whacking away at the Spaniards with that bleeding great cleaver he carried."

Sejanus shrugged. "You saw wrong. Must have been an indian, or a white man all smoked up."

So certain he was, John supposed himself mistaken, what with all the fire and blood and confusion.

They came in sight of Tortuga that afternoon, and there were wild cheers when her green mountains could be made out. Later men crowded the rail as they cruised along her south coast, watching for the little town by the lagoon, where a river came down to the sea. The late slanting sun made all the houses look as though they were on fire.

Yet Tortuga was growing peaceful these days, not so much a place of drunken mayhem as it had once been. A thoughtful governor had imported better than a thousand whores, to turn the attention of the populace to more domestic matters. Many of the buccaneers had married and settled down now, scratching out livings on little farms up the steep-sided canyons. Some had opened taverns and shops on the waterfront.

There was no harbor to speak of, so both *Harmony* and *Fraternity* moored off the lagoon and sent men ashore in the longboats. Captain Reynald went ashore briefly and returned with one M. Delahaye, a shabby-looking little man with spectacles. He led him on a tour of the *Harmony's* cargo deck to display her plunder. The two men talked affably together in French, as M. Delahaye made notes on a slate he carried with him, and at last he chalked up a figure and displayed it to Captain Reynald. Apparently Captain Reynald was pleased with the figure, for the two men embraced and went back ashore to seal their bargain with a friendly bottle of rum.

John watched wistfully from the rail, as the last of the crew prepared to go ashore.

"Reckon you'll be glad to see our backs, eh?" said Anslow, digging him in the ribs. "You and the missus get some privacy at last!"

John smiled and nodded. "To be sure," he said, thinking how winsomely the yellow lights of the town beckoned. There would have been good food ashore, and rum, and willing ladies to whom he'd have owed no debt but their set price.

"I don't know but that I oughtn't stay on board too," said Mr. Tudeley, perched indecisive on the rail.

"No, you want to go ashore and have a hell of a good time," said Anslow firmly, jerking his head at John and mouthing the words *Honeymoon, remember?* at Mr. Tudeley.

"You come on down, now," said Sejanus, laughing as he rose to help Mr. Tudeley into the boat. "Maybe there's a bookseller's stall here. Maybe there's a barber-surgeon to draw your tooth. Maybe there's a church! You won't know if you don't go see."

"I may as well," said Mr. Tudeley, with a sigh.

They rowed ashore. John turned, wondering whether in fact he might win back Mrs. Waverly's attention, if not her affections. He made his way down to their cabin, hefting a lantern, and found her emerging from the cabin with her arms full of bedding.

"Ah! There you are, Mr. James," said Mrs. Waverly. "I thought I'd take the opportunity to sleep in my old cabin tonight. I have so fearfully crowded you."

"Obliged," said John gruffly. He felt a strong urge for a stiff drink, but the rum was locked away on the orlop deck. "I reckon I'll sleep on deck, all the same, since there's just me to keep watch." He remembered Mr. Tudeley had been given some rum for his toothache, and wondered if there was any left. "Pardon me, ma'am." He edged past her and opened Mr. Tudeley's cabin, and thrust the lantern in.

Mr. Tudeley's trunk was standing open, his clothes and books strewn everywhere. John grimaced at the untidiness. "Landlubber," he muttered. He spotted the wooden tankard to one side and picked it up, but even before he opened the lid he could tell it was full. He tilted back the lid and peered in, and his mood brightened at once.

So he carried the rum up on deck, and sat there a while sipping it, looking up at the stars. He heard music coming from across the water, and sounds of raucous merriment from the little buildings with their yellow lights. It put him in a sentimental mood. He fell to thinking about Mrs. Waverly, and the way she'd wept for Tom Blackstone. He wondered whether any woman would weep for him when he should meet his end, whether he met it in battle or drowning in the green sea, or dying at a decent age in his brickyard...

He heard Henry Morgan's voice in his head, then, telling him sharply that he was becoming self-pitying sodden drunk. "Aye, sir," John said. He sighed, sitting upright and closing the lid of the tankard. He carried it belowdecks and set it back where he'd found it, in Mr. Tudeley's cabin. Then he thought he'd better get his hammock, so he edged down the passage and went into his cabin.

Preparing to unfasten the hammock, he took out the roll of folded sailcloth he'd been using as a pillow and tossed it on the deck. It landed with a hard sound, a sort of rattling tinkle; several objects spilled out of it. John peered down, surprised. Then he grabbed the lantern and held it down to see better.

There was a little pearl-handled knife. There was a ring. There was a sort of doll made of a carved nutshell, with a body of ribbon scraps and rags. There were three parrot feathers bound together with gold wire. There was a piece of heathen money with a hole in it. There was a whistle carved from a bone. All hidden in his pillow...

John heard his heart beating. His mouth was dry. Stone cold sober, he turned and opened the door.

Mrs. Waverly stood there, looking at him with narrowed eyes. He grabbed her hand and pulled her into the cabin.

"What's this, then?" he demanded. "What's this stuff doing in my gear? It was you took it, wasn't it, and hid it in my gear?"

She looked into his eyes a long moment, her gaze unfathomable; then she turned away and lifted her arm to hide her face. "Oh, God," she moaned, with tears choking her voice. "It has begun again. Oh, poor dear Mr. James, forgive me, please forgive me!"

John lessened his grip on her hand a bit. "What're you talking about?"

"They're only trifles. I meant no harm. I can't help myself—" Her tears were coming in full flood now. "Oh— Mr. James, I must—must throw myself on your mercy!"

John evened his breath, trying to calm himself at least. "First thing we got to do is put all this back," he said. "And it's a good job everyone else is ashore. Come on." He stooped and swept everything back into the pillow.

They went into the crew's quarters, with Mrs. Waverly whimpering and sobbing the whole while. She mastered herself enough to point mutely at each particular sea-chest, as John held up first one oddment and then another, so he could stow them back where they belonged. The whole time he listened hard, fearful of hearing footsteps creaking overhead that meant some of the crew had come back early. Once or twice he nearly told Mrs. Waverly to stop her noise, but gritted his teeth and forbore, realizing that rough treatment would only make her more hysterical.

When they were finished putting everything back, John took Mrs. Waverly by the hand and led her up on deck. "Now," he said, seating her on the helmsman's bench. "What in thunder did you steal all that trash for?"

"I don't know," said Mrs. Waverly, her voice rising shrilly. "I have never known. Oh, Mr. James, please don't tell! They were only petty, silly things, of no real value; and yet I should be so ashamed, if all those brave gentlemen thought less of me on that account."

"They'd likely do a bit worse than think less of you," said John. "I seen men flogged for doing what you done. You don't go thieving from your shipmates."

"But you're *pirates*," said Mrs. Waverly, looking genuinely confused. "You murdered everyone on that Spanish ship and stole their goods."

"Well—yes—yes, we did. But they was Spaniards, so it don't count."

"And before that, Captain Reynald and his crew stole the *Fyrey Pentacost*, whose crew were English!"

"Well, so they done, but he's a Frenchman. So it wasn't exactly like common thievery, see?"

"I see," said Mrs. Waverly, with a sniff. "*Common* thievery is the sticking point, then. I did think I might have found myself in the one society in which persons might be better disposed to excuse my little frailty."

"I'm sorry to say that ain't the case, ma'am," said John. "Your householder'll go and fetch a constable if he catches you stealing his goods, but your pirate won't bother with all that. He'll just pull out his knife and stick you a few times to make sure you don't go doing it again. D'you catch my meaning?"

Mrs. Waverly shuddered. "I suppose."

"And with you being a woman and all," John paused, uncertain how to phrase it delicately. "He's likeliest to pull something else out first, afore he goes for his knife."

Mrs. Waverly covered her face with her hands. "Oh, great God forbid!"

"How long have you been doing this?"

"I hadn't given offense in years," said Mrs. Waverly. "Oh, Mr. James, pity me! I am sure it is grief and the desperation of my present circumstance that has made it break out again. My father was old gentry in Hertfordshire—well-bred but improvident, and too trusting—we lost our manor and he died untimely, and we were obliged to go live with an aunt in London, in very mean circumstances—I think it began then.

"I am sure I do not know what possessed me. I could never recall how it had happened afterwards—all manner of oddments would be found in my apron pockets, or once or twice in my stockings. Spoons, mostly. Other people's thimbles. Hair ribbons. Nothing anyone would consider real *theft*, surely!

"And when I was happy and at peace, it would never happen at all. You see, do you not, Mr. James, that I am no malefactor?"

"Of course not," agreed John, though he was remembering Bess Whidbey who'd lived in the next street but one in Hackney, who'd been arrested coming out of a shop with a packet of brass pins hid in her bosom, and when they'd gone to her room they'd found row upon row of packets of pins lined up along the cupboard shelf, never opened, and her cool as ice the whole time declaring her innocence.

"Did Tom know about what you done?"

Mrs. Waverly nodded, weeping afresh. "Such a kind man—such an *understanding* man. He knew that I should die of shame were I ever caught out, and he protected me. And in truth, when dear Tom was alive I was seldom troubled. Will you not have mercy on an unhappy woman's weakness, Mr. James?" She reached out and clasped both his hands.

"Aw—" said John, and then her mouth was on his, she was grabbing his arms fit to leave finger-marks and pulling him down to her. He overbalanced and fell on one knee on the bench, which hurt considerably, but her mouth tasted of comfits and her little white teeth were raking his lip.

Except—

"Wait," he said, coming up for air with effort. "Wait. I thought you was sweet on Reynald. I ain't fighting no adultery duels with any Frenchman, especially when you and me ain't really married in the first place."

"Oh, Mr. James!" Mrs. Waverly tossed her head impatiently. "How can you imagine I should so demean myself as to dishonor Tom's memory with a person like Captain Reynald? I but play a role, as you do. Circumstance

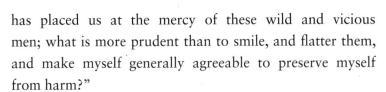

has placed us at the mercy of these wild and vicious men; what is more prudent than to smile, and flatter them, and make myself generally agreeable to preserve myself from harm?"

"You're not staying on in hopes of getting yourself some more earrings, then?"

"Sir!" said Mrs. Waverly, pulling away from him and sitting straight. "That insinuation is unworthy of you! One might as well ask why *you* have made no move to escape. We need but slip over the side, after all."

"Well," said John. "Where'd we go? The island is all bloody pirates. We'd only be leaving devils we know to trust ourselves with devils we don't. And anyone agrees to take us to Leauchaud for a price is going to want to know why we're going."

"You're not staying on because you find a brigand's life suits you?"

The shot hit home. John scowled at her.

"You can argue like a lawyer when you've a mind, can't you?"

"Of course I can. Consider, Mr. James: you are a *man*. You have at your disposal tremendous strength and courage with which to defend yourself, to say nothing of cutlasses and pistols. What have I, a weak and feeble woman, by comparison? Naught but my wit, my grace, my politesse!"

"True enough," said John, though he remembered a girl who had wielded a cutlass and pistol well enough and feared nothing. *Her* kiss had burned his mouth like white rum; and the memory of that gave him a bleak feeling, and suddenly he didn't feel like having Mrs. Waverly right there on the steersman's bench anymore.

"You'd best go below," he said, turning away from her and looking out at the lights of Tortuga. "I won't tell a soul what you done. You mustn't do it anymore, mind. Not as long as we're aboard this craft."

"You have my most fervent gratitude, Mr. James," said Mrs. Waverly, rising and adjusting her garments, which had become a little disheveled in their embrace. She wished him a pleasant goodnight and went below.

EIGHT:

Roistering

JOHN WOKE WITH THE sun in his eyes and the awareness of having heard a loud crash. He leaped up and fell sprawling from his hammock. The crash came again; something was striking the hull, amid a great deal of drunken laughter. He scrambled to his feet and went to look over the side.

One of the boats had come back from town. Mr. Tudeley lay unconscious in the bottom and Sam Anslow sprawled back on the oars, so their blade ends rose dripping from the sparkling sea. Sejanus was attempting to jump for a bit of knotted rope that hung down from the rail. As John watched, he caught it and pulled himself up, giggling.

"Good morning, sir!" he declared. "How was your delightful conjugal evening?" He fell over the rail.

"Hope yours is as nice," said John, feeling mean. "If you ever get a woman to marry you. What the hell happened to *him*?" He jerked his thumb downward at Mr. Tudeley.

His question provoked a fit of fresh laughter from Sejanus, and Anslow sat there snickering too.

"Oh, that's quite a story," said Sejanus, getting to his hands and knees. "Yes sir, that's what you'd call one of those epic stories. Where to begin. Where should we begin? How would you say we ought to begin, Mr. Anslow, sir?"

Mr. Anslow made a gurgling noise in reply.

"Well, sir," said Sejanus, pulling himself up on his knees via the rail. "Well. Little Mr. Tudeleley, or *Winty* as he asked us to call him—short for *Winthrop*, don't you know? He had this rotten tooth. We went ashore, he said, 'Oh, please, for the love of Jesus let us find a barber-surgeon to draw my tooth, before we do aught else'. So we were agreeable—weren't we agreeable, Mr. Anslow, sir?"

"Was," said Anslow.

"We searched high, we searched low, but no place could we find us a barber-surgeon," Sejanus continued. "So I said we ought to go drink some rum, as it might take the edge off Winty's toothache. And first he said he couldn't possibly, and then he said he really couldn't, and then he said, 'Oh, well, if you fellows are having some too I suppose a dram wouldn't hurt'. So we went to a little rum-shop and we set about drinking.

"By and by, this other fellow noticed Winty's groaning and swishing rum around on his tooth, and he asked what was the matter with him. We replied for Winty, didn't we, Mr. Anslow?"

"We did," said Anslow.

"And this man said, he said, 'Monsieur, I shall be happy to draw your tooth, in return for a drink.' I asked him was he a barber-surgeon and he said no, he was a blacksmith. Same thing really. And before Winty could do more than scream, Mr. Blacksmith had Winty's head under his arm and a pair of pliers out. Luckily—" Sejanus rose, with infinite care, to his feet and stood there swaying. "*Luckily,* one of us thought to stop him before he pulled out a tooth at random, and told Winty to point out the rotten one. Was it you thought to stop him, Mr. Anslow?"

"Naw," said Anslow.

"Why then, it must have been me. And, crack! Out came that tooth, and Winty was on his hands and knees on the floor spitting blood. So we picked him up and told him he was a brave hero. We bought rum for him, and the jolly blacksmith too. Little Winty liked the rum so well after that, he had another, and still another. By and by he said, 'Let's go roistering, my lads!'

"I said to him, I said, 'Define roistering for me, Winty, my man' and he replied with a word that is not generally used in polite company. And as I recall Mr. Anslow said— what was it you said, Mr. Anslow?"

"Hell yes," said Anslow.

"And we asked Brother Blacksmith if he knew where there was an establishment properly fitted up for the purpose Winty had in mind. Brother Blacksmith said 'Why, yes, indeed, I do know of such a place!' So we went there. We bought a bottle of rum to take with us, just in case there wasn't any where we were going.

"But it turned out the ladies kept a fine cellar full of good drink. Which was fortunate. I will draw the veil of discretion over what we did there, sir, but Winty astonished everyone by his fortitude. We could scarcely believe it, could we, Mr. Anslow?"

"Could have knocked me over with a feather," said Anslow.

"Even if we hadn't had those two other bottles," said Sejanus. "The ladies begged us to take him away, at last. They were exhausted by his company. They had to send out to the house down the lane for reinforcements. So we loaded Winty on a chair and carried him back. And here he is."

"You forgot the part about the tattoo," said Anslow.

"Bless me, so I did." Sejanus hiccupped. "Well. What do you think? Shall we pass a bight of rope around him, and haul him aboard?"

"We'd better," said John grimly.

So they brought Mr. Tudeley over the side. He never woke once during the process, so boneless that John and Sejanus had to carry him down to his cabin between them. Then Anslow fell into the sea while attempting to climb aboard, and they had to lower the rope and pull him out too.

"Rig a bosun's chair for the lady," he said, when he had come over the rail at last and lay there with a pool of seawater spreading around him.

"What lady?" asked John.

"One in the boat," said Anslow. "Sejanus's girl."

"There's no girl in the boat."

"Is so," said Mr. Anslow, and belched. "Pretty little neeg-a-ress. Powerful taken with him, she is. Come along with us in the boat."

"Well, she ain't there now," said John. Sejanus, who had stretched out in a triangle of shade and gone peacefully to sleep, was unavailable for comment.

"Awwww," said Anslow. He rolled on his side and went to sleep too.

All the ill-gotten gains of the cruise were unloaded over the next day or two, into flat-bottomed boats rowed out by M. Delahaye and his servants. Most men spent their share of the profits quickly, on rum and roistering (though Mr. Tudeley went no more ashore; his hoarse scream on discovering his tattoo had awakened half the ship). John prudently stowed his share, which amounted to about three pounds, in the bottom of his sea-chest. He still entertained ideas of quitting the life piratical and taking up his trade like an honest man, whatever Mrs. Waverly might say.

He did go so far as to venture ashore for an afternoon, and walk the lanes where he had once lost a fortune in a night, in days gone by. He tried to imagine himself setting up shop there. He even went into one or two grog shops, and looked around at their sandy floors to calculate how many bricks it'd take to do the common room. He tried to interest the landlords in making improvements to the premises, but they shrugged and shook their heads.

In the end he went back aboard the *Harmony*. He helped load the new stores aboard her, and did such an excellent and methodical job of stacking them, Captain Reynald appointed him Ship's Purser thereafter.

They stayed a month in that place, till all the money was spent. Then they hoisted sails and moved out, in search of more loot.

Mrs. Waverly did not resume her place in John's cabin, but kept to her own henceforth; and there was a lot of muttered talk about that, though more people were sympathetic to John than otherwise.

"Happens in every marriage," said Anslow, thumping him helpfully on the shoulder. "I been married three times, so I know. Once the honeymoon's past, they find all sorts of reasons to turn cold."

John just shrugged and said he reckoned so, and everyone complimented him for the stoicism with which he was taking things. He didn't much care what Mrs. Waverly was doing a'nights, having concluded that she was a bit too sharp for his liking. Her mania for stealing oddments put him off too.

There was no further talk of that, at least. No one mentioned that their lost goods had been found again, though that was likely due to a disinclination to admit they'd simply misplaced things rather than had them stolen. John was grateful. Still on thinking it over he remembered how Mrs. Waverly had stowed her little trifles in *his* bedding rather than her own, and that further armored his heart against her charms.

NINE:

Foxes and Wolves

"**H**OLD ON TO THE shroud and put your feet on the ratlines," John advised. "And don't look down."

"And which are the shrouds, pray, and which the ratlines?" inquired Mr. Tudeley, with a peevish glance aloft.

"The shrouds is the upright bits; the ratlines is what'd be rungs, if it was a ladder," said John.

"Then why not call them rope ladders and be plain?" snapped Mr. Tudeley. He bore little resemblance now to the meek clerk who had come aboard the *Fyrey Pentacost*. He wore no shirt at the moment, having been advised that the quickest way to make his tattoo less noticeable was to acquire a tan. He was unshaven, red-eyed, with a prominent gap in the teeth of his lower jaw. His spectacles were bound on his head with string, and his graying hair stuck out on either side of the bind, over his right ear and the scabbed stump of his left ear. He gave off a pronounced smell of rum when he exhaled, for he had acquired the habit of taking a dram at intervals to calm his nerves.

"A ship has its own language, like," said John.

"Sounds like damn'd idiocy," said Mr. Tudeley, grabbing hold of the ratlines and starting up toward the crosstrees. "Oh, Jesus Christ, and I'm expected to mount upward like this in such a gale? I am a Job, a very Job, sir, that's what I am. Is there no end to my suffering?"

"This ain't a gale," said John, smiling involuntarily. "This is just brisk. I'm coming up behind you, so you needn't fear falling. You'll get used to this so you run up and down just as though it was stairs at home, you mark my words."

"'*At home*' you say? What home have I? Shunted from one place to another, all my bloody life, ever since I left school. The wife and I took a pretty little cottage on Hampstead Heath; she committed adultery with our landlord, and he had the effrontery to tell *me* to look for other lodgings, if you please! I lived in one wretched lodging-house after another until coming to the West Indies, and what a sty I was given for residence on that plantation! And to what had I to look forward at my sister's, even supposing this filthy chance had not afflicted us, but a spare bed made up in a dusty corner of a gable?"

Spleen carried him as high as the crosstrees, where he paused, peering upward at the lubber's hole and futtock-shrouds.

"Don't go through the lubber's hole there," said John. "That's only for—er—lubbers. Climb up around the outside, leaning backwards and hanging onto the futtock-shrouds to pull yourself over the edge of the top. That's how a real mariner does it."

Mr. Tudeley stared up openmouthed.

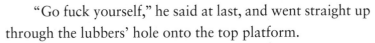

"Go fuck yourself," he said at last, and went straight up through the lubbers' hole onto the top platform.

"There ain't any need to be uncivil," said John, following him up over the futtock-shrouds.

"What's a lifetime of civility ever gotten me?" said Mr. Tudeley, who had wrapped his arms and legs around the join where the topmast was fished to the mast and clung there like a limpet.

"Not killed afore now?" John stood up and surveyed the wide horizon. There was, as he had said, a brisk breeze, and the *Harmony* cruised along pleasantly. Only, far off to the east, was a smudge of some dirty color.

"Ha! I should welcome the quietus, sir. Here am I, obliged to wear spectacles after a lifetime of ruining mine eyes on copy-work, and who does the captain send up to keep lookout? Who but I, fortune's whipping-boy? It makes no *sense!*"

"Things don't make sense, much," said John. "On the other hand, you ain't any use at hauling and you don't know the ropes. I reckon Captain Reynald is being charitable-like finding you something you can do. It ain't so bad. All you have to do is watch all round the horizon, and sing out if you see a sail."

"And meanwhile live up here exposed to the wind and the rain like a sodding stylite," said Mr. Tudeley. "Though I suppose if you can bear your present lot, sir, I must bear mine."

"What's that mean?"

"Pardon me, sir, but the disgraceful behavior of Mrs. Waverly cannot have escaped your notice," said Mr. Tudeley. "Why, I happed upon her yestereen in Captain Reynald's arms, when I went up to relieve myself at moonrise."

"Oh," said John, surprised to feel a throb of jealousy. "I didn't mean that. I know she's been making sheep's eyes at him. And he at her, come to that. I reckon she's using her court-ways to get herself some more presents of emeralds. Much I care; like I told you, she's only the widow of my mate at Panama. Nothing to me."

"Then you are wise," said Mr. Tudeley. "What did you mean, then?"

"About what? Oh. What's a stylite?"

"A saint given to mortifying his flesh by living atop a high pillar," Mr. Tudeley explained. "Abjuring any earthly pleasure, fasting and praying, and never setting foot on solid ground for years together. The simile is apt, I think."

John decided not to ask him what a simile was. "Ah. Fancy that."

The breeze changed its quarter and grew stronger suddenly, buffeting them. Its freshness had all gone; it was hot, like a wind out of an oven door. John turned his head to the east, out of which the wind had come. He watched the dirty smudge, and thought it looked as though it had spread up the sky a bit.

"Perhaps the Lord intended me to be a stylite," said Mr. Tudeley. "Certainly I have not been destined for earthly happiness. God knows I have suffered constant mortification. I wonder whether that will mitigate in my favor, when I stand before the Throne of Judgment?"

"Maybe," said John, feeling a prickle of sweat as the temperature went shooting up. Mr. Tudeley took out a filthy handkerchief, mopped his brow, and observed:

"There's a sail over there."

"What? Where?"

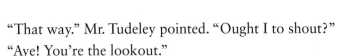

"That way." Mr. Tudeley pointed. "Ought I to shout?"

"Aye! You're the lookout."

"Halllooo! I see a ship!"

"No, you stupid—Ahoy! Sail to larboard!"

"Well, that's certainly set them to scurrying about like ants," said Mr. Tudeley. He put his handkerchief away and unlooped a little bellarmine jug from his belt, in which he carried his rum ration. He uncorked it and had a thoughtful pull. "I suppose now we'll assail some innocent vessel, slaughter her sailors, and take her cargo?"

"That's the general idea," said John uneasily. Both the stain on the sky and the unknown ship were moving quickly. The ship was now hull-up over the horizon and making straight for the *Harmony,* showing no inclination to evade her. Looking down, he saw Captain Reynald opening his spyglass to have a look at the strange vessel.

The captain regarded her in silence a long while, as gleeful men ran around him getting ready for the attack. They loaded small arms and piled them up, and brought up a coil of slow-match to portion out to the gunners. A whetstone was passed from hand to hand, as men put edges on their blades and boarding axes.

Captain Reynald closed up his glass with a snap. "Belay! We run, gentlemen. We are foxes, but they are wolves. Make the sail!"

"What d'you mean?" John heard Anslow demanding. Captain Reynald held out his spyglass with an ironical expression. Anslow stepped into view from where he'd been obscured by the mainsail and took it to see for himself. John saw him peering out at the oncoming stranger. John turned round and looked hard. He was young then

and his eyes were sharp; he could just make out the tri-
colored flag.

"Oh bugger," he said. "It's a bloody Dutchman."

"Is it?" Mr. Tudeley had another drink of rum. "Have
they anything we want?"

"A lot of guns, by the look of her," said John unhappily.
Men were scrambling up into the *Harmony's* rigging as fast
as they could go to let out sail, and the little *Fraternity* had
already changed course and was skipping away like a hare.

"One side!" shouted a topman, shoving past John to
run out on the yard.

"Guns," said Mr. Tudeley in a meditative voice. "That
would be cannons, am I correct?"

"Aye."

"Of which we have only that swivel gun on the rail?"

"Aye."

"Seems rather an oversight on Captain Reynald's part,
doesn't it?"

"I reckon he's been counting on speed and the sharp-
shooters, like he done when he took us," said John. The Dutchman
still came on, bearing down on the *Harmony*, who spread her
full compliment of sail at last and, tacking, took off after the
Fraternity. Mr. Tudeley clutched the mast, closed his eyes and
swore under his breath as they came about. John gripped hard
on the topmast shrouds as they swung through the full arc, too
busy looking back at the Dutchman to mind the sway.

She seemed too orderly and clean for a pirate, but there
was a lean hungry look to her that didn't square with John's
notions of a Dutch West India ship. Clearly she meant to give
chase, though; for she was unfurling more of her canvas and
swinging her bow to follow the *Harmony*.

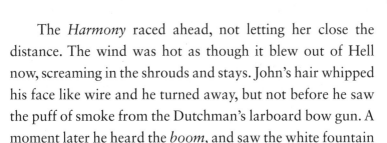

The *Harmony* raced ahead, not letting her close the distance. The wind was hot as though it blew out of Hell now, screaming in the shrouds and stays. John's hair whipped his face like wire and he turned away, but not before he saw the puff of smoke from the Dutchman's larboard bow gun. A moment later he heard the *boom*, and saw the white fountain leap up in the *Harmony's* wake.

"Damn," said John. "She's getting our range."

"I expect we're doomed, then," said Mr. Tudeley in a dull voice. He still had his eyes screwed tight shut.

"Maybe not," said John, "Maybe not. All them guns ain't half heavy. We're lighter and God knows we can run."

Mr. Tudeley made no reply, but groped for his jug and drank more rum.

The *Fraternity* ran, and the *Harmony* ran, and the Dutchman pursued them hard, though she seemed unable to close within range for her shots to count for anything. She left off shooting after awhile and just came on, grim and silent as a mastiff. She never tried to hail them; she never ran up any other colors.

"What do you suppose they want?" asked Mr. Tudeley, finishing his rum.

"Could be hunting pirates," said John. "Just to kill us. Could be scavenging for what they can get. No way to tell 'em we haven't got anything worth taking just now, though, if that's the case." He glanced over his shoulder and saw, with a shock, that the discoloration on the sky was now overarching, as though they had sped backward across the curve of the world. The sea was greened copper. The air was hot as a furnace.

John looked down and saw Mrs. Waverly standing in

the companionway, watching Captain Reynald as he paced to and fro. Sejanus was at the rail with three or four others, staring back at the Dutchman. John blinked and stared, and rubbed his eyes and stared again. There was another black, or at least a mulatto, standing beside Sejanus. He wore the clothes of a common sailor, and was watching not the Dutchman but Sejanus himself, who seemed to be taking no notice of him.

Captain Reynald went to the companionway and crouched down, saying something to Mrs. Waverly. She smiled bravely and said something back. He looked over his shoulder and then kissed her. John felt a knot in his heart, but he turned away. *Nothing to me,* he told himself.

The sea was rising. They could look out on the long swell, mountains of water rolling skyward. The *Fraternity* disappeared and reappeared, behind one mountain and the next. The Dutchman kept on after them like a charging bull, but even she seemed to labor now in the troughs of the waves. White water broke, and ran over the deck; John looked down again and saw Sejanus standing alone at the rail.

Mr. Tudeley said something, lifting a feeble arm to point to larboard, and John realized he had gone quite deaf for the shrieking of the wind. He looked where Mr. Tudeley was pointing and saw a dark coastline. He filled his lungs and bawled "Land ho! Land to starboard! Lee shore!"

He could hear his own voice at least, and it carried to the deck below. Captain Reynald's head went up; he glanced to larboard and began screaming orders out, just as the first hot rain hit John in the face like a pailful of shot. He gasped and wiped his face, but the rain kept coming, in sheets, and all was gleaming-wet on board the *Harmony* now. Fearful

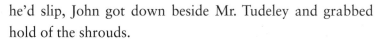
he'd slip, John got down beside Mr. Tudeley and grabbed hold of the shrouds.

"Oughtn't we to put into land?" cried Mr. Tudeley.

"No!" John yelled back. "We'd run aground and wreck!"

"Well, at least we'd be on dry land—"

"In little pieces!" John looked around for the *Fraternity,* but couldn't make her out anywhere. Color had been drained away: the sea was white, the sky and driving water were white, beaten foam flying and spattering. He glanced behind then, shielding his face with one hand, and thought he saw the Dutchman ploughing nose-down into a wave. Then he was blinded, as the world erupted in a blast of purple-white light, and deafened as thunder clapped down on them like a physical blow.

When he raised his face, black rain-glistening figures were swarming all around, topmen leaving the rigging, seeming to flow like snakes down the sheets and shrouds. Dazedly he pulled at Mr. Tudeley's shoulder.

"We got to get down!"

"No!" Mr. Tudeley clung like a limpet to his perch. "No!"

"We'll get struck!" ·

"No!"

"I'm not staying!"

"No!"

Giving up, John groped over the edge for the futtock-shrouds and swung himself down. In his descent he was tilted far over one way, so that for a second he lay prone on the shrouds, and then so far the other way he was swung out in the air hanging on by his hands only, as his feet kicked the clouds of flying water. He expected any moment for

Mr. Tudeley's body to come hurtling past him, but it never happened. When his feet found the chains at last he peered up and glimpsed Mr. Tudeley up there still, silhouetted by a flash of lightning, screaming curses at God or Fate or the sea.

Waves warm as bathwater were breaking over the deck now, sheets of foam pocked by the relentless rain, and the high squealing wind was no less loud down on deck. John groped his way down from the chains and hung on to the rail. Sodden figures clung to anything standing, gasping for air as each wave receded, putting their heads down to endure the next that swept over them; he saw three men at the tiller, straining with bared teeth to steer a course, but he knew the *Harmony* must be driven ashore now. He looked around to see it he could make out the coastline, but another flash of lightning came.

When John opened his dazzled eyes he saw the rock, the only black and steady thing in that churning surging white nightmare. There it was to starboard. The *Harmony* seemed to dance round it. There it was to larboard, and then the *Harmony* struck, with a sound louder than the thunder or the wind, the loudest sound John had ever heard in his life, the rending splintering crunch that meant it was over.

He was choking under water in the scuppers. He rolled over into air, peering up the deck which sloped above him steep as a mountainside. He began to scale it, hand over hand, past other soaked and struggling men. A wave the size of a house came over them, scouring down the deck. John caught hold of the edge of the companionway and held on. When he came up for air and drank in breath, he found himself staring into Mrs. Waverly's gray eyes. Her face was white, her hair down around her shoulders, streaming like amber seaweed.

"I will not die in there," she said, inaudibly but John read her lips. She looked beyond him and John turned to see what she was staring at.

Sejanus and the mulatto were working at the ship's boat, unlashing it from its cradle. No one was attempting to stop them, or help them; every man left on deck was making his slow determined way hand over hand to the companionway, shoving past Mrs. Waverly as they flopped inside.

"Anslow!" roared John, as Anslow slid past him. "The boat!"

Anslow shook his head, with a sick grin. "The rum," he said, and vanished below, to get as drunk as he might before the sea got him. Mrs. Waverly screamed and John half-rolled to see another wave coming at the *Harmony,* charging at her bows, spume high as a cathedral, a white cliff looming. It took forever to break, but when it did it lifted the bow of the Harmony, tilting her on her beam-end before dropping her with a crash as it flooded over the deck. Sejanus, the mulatto and the boat all vanished in a confusion of shattered water and noise; John looked up and saw the prow of the boat coming at him. He grabbed it and shoved it away. The water receded and the *Harmony* settled again with a grinding lurch. The boat lay in the scuppers with Sejanus rolling in it He looked stunned, struggled feebly.

Mrs. Waverly pushed herself from the companionway and slid down the deck to the boat. John let go and slid after her. He could hear planks splitting now, and a crack as the fore topmast broke and came crashing down, trailing all its rope and blocks. Mrs. Waverly scrambled nimbly over the gunwale into the boat and John hauled himself in after her. He lay there exhausted a moment, looking at her wet bare legs. She screamed again but the wave broke before he could raise his head to see it, a ton of white water smothering and blinding him, and he felt the boat pitch as the wave sluiced it clean off the deck and into the sea.

The motion changed at once. John opened his eyes and found the boat swamped and wallowing. Mrs. Waverly and Sejanus had risen to their knees and were baling with their cupped hands. John followed their example, there under the high black shadow of the *Harmony*. The oars had gone; he saw one floating away, nearly close enough to reach but not without pitching himself out of the boat. A bucket did go bobbing by and Sejanus was able to grab it, and resumed baling.

Another sharp crack, and a rending noise. John glanced over his shoulder and saw the *Harmony's* mainmast going over, falling toward them. It seemed to be shrieking as it came. John spotted Mr. Tudeley, clinging until the impact of the fall shook him loose like an insect. He dropped into the water and sank. A moment later his bellarmine jug, and then his head, broke the surface and he was yowling and spitting, flailing in the water. John and Sejanus put out their hands and hauled him into the boat. He sat huddled on a thwart, shivering, glaring at them.

A sudden beam of flaming light shone all around. The falling rain looked like drops of fire. They in the boat raised their heads, bewildered, and saw the red band of light at the far horizon, where the sun was setting in blood. It illuminated the wreck of the *Harmony*, on whose vertical deck not a man could be seen: her trailing tattered sails, her snapped yards and cordage all hanging down abandoned. She rolled like a dying animal, groaning. Her bowsprit stabbed into the wet air.

The boat bobbed aimlessly a moment and then began to move away from her, as a current took it. They were pulled around, circling the rock, and away. The sun winked out and for a little while there was a glow that marked where it had been, like a bed of coals. Then it was dark, unrelieved by any star. They were adrift on the wide night ocean, ascending mountains and descending valleys of sullen black water.

TEN:

A Bawdy Catch

OR A WHILE THEY took turns baling, until the rain stopped at last John's hearing returned by degrees, as the ringing faded from his ears. They rode the surge up and down.

"Have we any rum?" said Mr. Tudeley at last.

"No," said Sejanus.

"What about food or water?"

"No."

There was a lengthy silence, and at last Mr. Tudeley said: "I have read, in some books, that savages in the tropics will leap from their canoes into the water, when they spy a great fish swimming thereunder, and stab it with their knives and wrestle it back into the canoe. Would you perhaps give that a try, sir?"

"I was born in Massachusetts," said Sejanus wearily. "I can dig for clams. If I have a clam rake."

"Oh. I see." Mr. Tudeley sounded petulant. "Well. Perhaps it won't be necessary. Perhaps we're near land.

I descried land off to the west, at least I think it was the west, shortly before we wrecked. Had anyone listened to me and steered for it, I daresay we might now be at a secure anchorage in some pleasant harbor. May I say, Mr. James, that you owe me an apology for your contemptuous dismissal of my suggestion?"

"Oh, shut your mouth," said John. He couldn't make out the change in Mr. Tudeley's features, in the dark, but he felt the lurch as Mr. Tudeley sprang to his feet.

"Damn you, sir! I shan't be spoken to in that manner, do you hear me?" Mr. Tudeley screamed, and sprang forward with his fists raised. "Not by you nor any other grinning ruffian, ever again!"

Perhaps he meant to fling himself on John. John thrust out his open hand, with rather more force than he had meant to use, and caught Mr. Tudeley square in the chest. Mr. Tudeley teetered back and stepped with both feet on the gunwale of the boat. There he danced a long second, his arms windmilling frantically as he tried to regain his balance while the boat tilted dangerously to that side. Both John and Sejanus threw themselves forward to grab him, and collided. Their combined weight was enough to capsize the boat. John heard Mrs. Waverly say a word he hadn't thought ladies knew, before he went under the dark water.

He broke the surface with a harsh gasp and looked about frantically for the boat. It glimmered faintly a little way off, keel upmost, and if it hadn't been painted white he'd have missed it. He swam for his life and caught hold, dragging himself up its side just as a pair of white arms appeared from the other side, clawing and grasping. He nearly yelled in horror, thinking it was a sea-phantom; but it was only Mrs. Waverly. She caught hold of his hands.

"Where are the others?" she asked.

"Don't know," said John.

"Here I am," said Sejanus out of the near darkness, and after a moment's splashing he found them and grabbed hold of the keel. "Did we lose Winty?"

"Good riddance," growled John.

"Damn your eyes, you whoreson dog," said Mr. Tudeley, who had swum up beside him.

"Mr. Tudeley!" said Mrs. Waverly.

"If you please, Winty," said Sejanus, with his white teeth flashing in the darkness, "Remember there is a lady present."

"Oh, sod off," said Mr. Tudeley. "My apologies, ma'am, I'm sure."

They tried to right the boat, four or five times, without success; exhausted as they were, at last they desisted and merely pulled themselves as far up the boat's hull as they could manage, and clung on to the keel. Presently Mr. Tudeley said he couldn't feel his hands anymore.

"I can see them," he said, "But it's as though they belonged to someone else. They're starting to slip. I shan't be able to hold fast much longer, and I don't believe I'll be able to lift my arms to swim, if it comes to that. I'll drop straight to the bottom, like a lead plumb bob. Unless that a shark—"

"You stop your noise or I'll drown you myself," said John.

"Gentlemen," said Mrs. Waverly, in a supernaturally calm voice, "If you don't cease quarreling at once, I shall begin to scream. I shall scream and scream. In truth, I don't believe I shall be able to stop screaming. And you shall face the choice of either drowning yourselves, or enduring being trapped on an overturned boat with a ceaselessly screaming female. Have I made myself quite plain?"

"Yes, ma'am," they all replied.

"How nice. Sejanus, could I trouble you to catch hold of Mr. Tudeley's wrists, in order to keep him from slipping off the boat? And he in turn shall anchor you. Thank you. Mr. James, would you please hold my wrists in the same manner? Very good. And now, gentlemen, I shall teach you all a merry and diverting catch to pass the time."

"What?" said John.

"We are going to keep our spirits up by singing," said Mrs. Waverly, a hint of steel in her manner once more.

"I have sung my last damned hymn," declared Mr. Tudeley.

"It isn't a hymn, Mr. Tudeley. It is quite indecent. My late husband learned it from a drinking companion at Oxford. It is a song, in fact, about an ugly woman. Now, which of you is a baritone?"

Nobody answered, and presently she warned "I'll start screaming…"

"I'm a tenor!" said Sejanus.

"I'm a countertenor!" said Mr. Tudeley.

"Well, what's a baritone sound like?" said John, who had sung in the choir at St. Augustine's as a boy but found more interesting pastimes once his testicles had descended.

"Deep, like a bull. I think you're a baritone or a bass," said Sejanus.

"I suspect he is too," said Mrs. Waverly. "Now then, Mr. James, I shall teach you the first part of the catch.

"Taking his beer with old Anacharsis
Quoth surly Swashbuckler, 'Your wife, sir, mine arse is!'"
"Madam!" said Mr. Tudeley, appalled. Sejanus chuckled.
"Sing it, Mr. James!"

John repeated it, fearful of her tone, some three or four times before they all agreed he had the melody pat.

"Now, Mr. Tudeley, it will fall to you to sing the lines of the ancient philosopher. I am sure you'll prove equal to the task.

"'Vous avez,' quoth Sage, 'she's a homely brown lass,
But after a bumper or two she might pass.'"

With trembling voice, Mr. Tudeley sang the verse after her. He was indeed a countertenor.

"What a delightful voice, Mr. Tudeley! And yet I am sure you have never had the benefit of a surgeon."

"I am fully intact, I assure you, ma'am," said Mr. Tudeley, rallying a little.

"What a pleasant thought. Now, Sejanus, here is your verse:

"Th' advice was so right it converted Sir Knight
Who all his life after drank Saturday night."

Sejanus sang the tenor part clearly.

"*Very* good, gentlemen! Now, in a round, if you please."

Hands joined over the keel, they sang the bawdy old catch, and their voices echoed out across the night. After about the fifth repetition John got the joke, and roared his verse lustily as though he sat by a sea-coal fire in Hackney, with a pint-jack of ale in his fist.

They sang it until they were thoroughly weary of it, and then Mrs. Waverly led them in a song about a courtier and a shepherdess, and when they had worn that out John taught them *Will You Buy Some of My Fish,* and later Mr.

Tudeley—to everyone's astonishment—taught them a song to the tune of *The Vicar of Bray* that had nothing whatsoever to do with matters ecclesiastical.

The sea grew still. At some hour in the long night the cloud-rack broke up, and stars glimmered through. A sliver of crescent appeared down near the horizon, sending a white trail of reflection across the water.

At some point thereafter, Mr. Tudeley's rendition of *The Stinking Tinker* broke off in a hoarse shriek of terror. The others, startled, scrambled as far up the hull as they could manage. John watched Mr. Tudeley, expecting to see him pulled below the surface. Sejanus tightened his grip; but Mr. Tudeley continued to hang there, with a curious expression on his face.

"I believe I'm standing on something," he said.

And in the silence that followed his remark, John heard what he had not noticed over their music, in the last few minutes: the sound of breakers, beating close by in the night. Now that he looked up and around, he saw that his companions were visible in the gloom, that the night had drained away into pallor, and a dark mass of land lay before them.

It transpired that Mr. Tudeley was standing on a submerged rock. As the light grew greater they saw many black spires and lumps of rock protruding from the sea, with cloudy surges boiling around them. Somehow they guided the overturned boat past, swimming, threading the maze to a narrow crescent of stone-studded beach.

Once on the sand they were able to right the boat at last. John and Sejanus had to go down on all fours and shove it along with their shoulders, to get it above the tideline; they had lost all strength in their hands to grip, after so many hours of clinging on. Mrs. Waverly and Mr. Tudeley stumbled ahead of them, making for a grove of palm trees. There they sat down, plump, upon a sort of lawn of coarse grasses.

"We're saved," Mr. Tudeley croaked. Mrs. Waverly only nodded, too weary to speak. John and Sejanus got the boat safely on dry land, with a last grunt of effort, and collapsed on either side in the sand. John lay his head on his arm, meaning to rest for a moment before getting up to spy out where they might be.

ELEVEN:

Dead Men

WHEN NEXT JOHN KNEW anything there was a hot sun burning his legs. He lifted his head and blinked, dazzled by a confusion of greens and whites and blues that resolved into the beach and grove in the full light of noon. His head burned; he had a raging thirst.

He sat up. Sejanus had crawled far enough forward to be lying in the shade. Mr. Tudeley was curled on his side under a palm tree, clutching a coconut to his bosom. Both men were snoring. John looked around for Mrs. Waverly. He saw only a line of footprints trailing away up the beach.

"Oi!" He scrambled to his feet. Sejanus lifted his head and looked around. Mr. Tudeley sat up blearily. "Where's she got to?"

They followed the footprints down the beach. "Doesn't look as though she was carried off by anyone," said Sejanus. "She wasn't running, either."

"What would she run off for?" said John, thinking uneasily of Tom's letter and the four thousand pounds.

"Where do you suppose we are?" inquired Mr. Tudeley, trailing behind them. He was still clutching his coconut. "The Spanish Main, perhaps?"

"I wouldn't have thought we'd run that far," said Sejanus.

"How does one open one of these, do you suppose?" Mr. Tudeley turned the coconut round in his hands.

"There she is!" John broke into a run. Mrs. Waverly had come around a low hill, walking back toward them. She carried a bucket. John, reaching her well ahead of the others, said: "You didn't ought to go off on your own like that. No telling where we are. There might be savages."

"There aren't," Mrs. Waverly replied, in a colorless voice. Her eyes were red; she had been weeping. "We're on an island. We are alone here, save for the dead."

"The dead?"

She turned and pointed back the way she had come. "They're all along the beach. Some from the *Harmony*, and others I didn't recognize. Perhaps they were from the Dutch ship. There is a great deal of wreckage. We ought to try to salvage it." She looked down at the bucket she carried, and held it up. "And I found a spring of water. We shan't die of thirst, at least. I brought you a drink."

John grabbed the bucket and gulped the water down before remembering his manners. He wiped his mouth on his sleeve and muttered hasty thanks. Sejanus and Mr. Tudeley got to them at last.

"Drank it all yourself, did you, you brute?" said Mr. Tudeley, in indignation. John handed him the empty bucket.

"Fetch more yourself. Where's the spring?" He turned to Mrs. Waverly.

"Just around the hill. You'll find it," she replied. "I believe I'll go gather fallen coconuts, shall I?"

She walked away from them without another word. They stared after her a moment, and then went carefully around the headland, wading part of the way.

A long expanse of beach opened out before them on the other side. John, shading his eyes from the glare with his hand, squinted into the distance and saw that there were indeed dead men lying all along the line of the tide, and others tumbling in the surf. Far down he thought he saw a broken mast sticking up, from rocks just offshore, but whose it might be he could not tell.

They walked forward in silence, until Mr. Tudeley spotted the spring coming down from the cliff to one side and made for it with a cry. They drank greedily, all three, scooping the water up in their hands when they couldn't bring themselves to wait for the bucket to fill.

"I reckon we ought to go on and see," said John at last. Sejanus nodded and they walked on, once more following Mrs. Waverly's footprints. She had zigzagged along, going down to the water here and there to pull barrels or lengths of rope up on the sand. Here she had paused by Anslow's body and turned him over, but gulls had already lighted on him and begun to peck at his eyes. John chased them away and pulled Anslow's shirt up to cover the face.

"We'll need to bury them," said Sejanus.

"What with?"

Sejanus shrugged. He found a broken oar and hefted it. They walked on. Mrs. Waverly's footprints veered away from the dead men, for a great distance after that, until they came to Captain Reynald's body.

He lay with one arm flung out, as though pointing. They could see where she'd knelt beside him for a while; the print of her gown was quite distinct in the damp sand, where she'd dragged him from the surf. The gulls hadn't started on him yet and he looked young and handsome, almost as though he was sleeping.

They stood there looking at him a while. John didn't know what he was supposed to feel. Satisfaction, maybe, that the man was dead; but then again he'd no claim himself to Mrs. Waverly's affections, had he? Besides, Captain Reynald had been good at his chosen trade. *You have to honor a man for that*, thought John.

They pulled the body a bit farther up from the tide, and covered its face, before they walked on. Where shelving rocks ran out into the water, all grown over in sea anemones and mussels, they saw that there was indeed a splintered mast tilting up. There was most of a ship there, all broken to pieces, the Dutchman by the look of her. Kegs and crates floated in the tidepools, bobbing in the surge. Mr. Tudeley found a man's shirt floating in a pool, and wrung it out and tried it on; it fit him, so he wore it. Sejanus found a length of calico in a tangle of weed, and so they tore it between them and made kerchiefs to tie on their heads against the sun. A little farther on there was another oar, which John picked up.

They spent a while wading back and forth, salvaging. There were more bodies caught in the kelp there, smashed up pretty badly. Where a moat of clear water floated around a standing rock they found a black man dead, looking up from the bottom as from a bath.

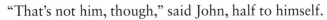
"That's not him, though," said John, half to himself.

"Who?" said Sejanus.

"The mulatto that was helping you loose the boat."

"Nobody helped me get the boat," said Sejanus sharply. "There weren't any mulattos on board."

"But I saw him, too," said Mr. Tudeley. "I tell you he was there, sir."

"You didn't see anyone," said Sejanus. "There was no one there to see."

"Now, don't you make game with us, mate," said John. "There was that big one with the sword, when we took the *Santa Ysabel*. There was a black girl at Tortuga, which I didn't see, but poor Anslow that's dead saw her plain. And then we saw the mulatto helping you with the boat. So don't you tell me they weren't there!"

Sejanus glared at them. "Chah! Where'd they go, then?" he said. "Where'd they disappear to, if they were real? You tell me that."

And any other man might have struggled to come up with an answer that made sense, and failed, and looked away sheepishly. But John had once seen a pretty girl turn into a ravening spirit of war, right before his eyes in broad daylight, and he knew there were answers that made no kind of sense to a reasoning man.

"I'll tell you what it is," he said. "This is some of your heathen gods, ain't it?"

"I don't have any gods," said Sejanus. "Didn't I tell you I was an atheist? And they aren't gods, anyway."

"What d'you call them, then?" said John, in triumph. "You *did* see them, and you're a liar if you say you didn't."

Sejanus looked away and made a sour face. "They're

called loas. My mama called them orishas. Just spirits, not gods. Spirits of places; spirits of things. We left them behind in Africa. The obeah-people bargained with them like pedlars, trading them food and drink and I don't know what, in return for favors.

"My old father was an obeah man. But when the big ship took him away from Africa, the loas couldn't even cross the water with him. Couldn't make his chains drop off, either. Not much use, eh?"

"But they must have made it across," said John, "Or they wouldn't be haunting you now."

"There are no loas here," Sejanus insisted.

"But we saw them," said Mr. Tudeley, who was only just managing to follow the conversation. "Are they devils?"

"No! They're only imaginary. I imagined them."

"But *we saw them too*," said John.

"That's only because I imagine better than white folks can," said Sejanus sullenly. He stuck the end of his oar into the sand. "These will do for shovels. Let's start burying all these bodies, before they can stink up the place."

They buried as many as they had strength for then, and hauled the others above the waterline to bury later. John dug deeper for Anslow than for the others, because he'd known him longer. Anslow was rolled into his grave and John stood there a moment, trying to recall a prayer to say. All he could think of was that he always seemed to draw burial detail. On consideration, he decided he'd rather be the one doing the shoveling than the poor bastard being shoveled under, like Anslow.

When they came back to the grove at last, they found that Mrs. Waverly had indeed gathered coconuts for them, and moreover waded out into the rock pools and gathered whelks, using a knife she had apparently found on one of the bodies.

"Did you salvage much of the wreck?" she inquired coolly, gouging a whelk from its shell.

"Some," said John, picking up a coconut and wishing he'd thought to take Anslow's knife before he'd buried him.

"I noticed a great deal of wood. We ought to be able to fashion new oars for the boat, and escape," she said.

"We'll need to do better than that," said John. "I been adrift in an open boat. No shelter, no safe place to keep victuals. We want something bigger. I was thinking we could build something from the wreckage. A pinnace, maybe. We could rig it with a sail. Lots of sailcloth washing about."

"Better still." She smiled at him, for the first time in days. She glanced over at Mr. Tudeley and Sejanus, who were attempting to open a coconut, and spoke in a lower voice: "It may be that we shall resume our journey to Leauchaud after all. Only think of that!"

John thought of it, and weighed up matters in his head. Much as he'd enjoyed being back on the account again, there was no denying he was once more penniless and at loose ends, and after nearly drowning at that. He saw in his mind a shopfront with his name above the door, and a yard full of good red brick, and all those folk needing new premises built in Port Royal. It put him in a generous mood.

"I'm sorry about Reynald," he said. "I know you liked him."

She shrugged, but did not look away from slicing up the whelk. "He seemed a decent man. A pity he drowned; but such was the risk of his profession, was it not? Nor will all the tears in the world bring him back. Let us go on and live." She lifted the raw whelk and bit into it with her white teeth, and chewed.

"I think you're hitting it on the wrong end," Sejanus advised Mr. Tudeley. "There's supposed to be three little eyes, somewhere."

"I don't see any," said Mr. Tudeley. He raised a stone and brought it down on the coconut like a hammer, only to hit his thumb.

"I reckon you've lost Tom's letter now," said John to Mrs. Waverly. "I hope you recollect what was in it, about where the money was hid?"

She looked pained. "My dear Mr. James, every word of that letter is written on my heart. Pray, have no concern on that account."

"Yeeeeeaaaaarrrgh!" Mr. Tudeley, losing patience, flung the coconut as hard as he could against a rock. It struck with the sound of a cutlass cleaving a skull. He snatched it up and pressed his lips to the cracked shell, sucking avidly at the milk.

TWELVE:

Wrecks

THERE WAS AN OPEN meadow on the slope above the spring, and there they made a camp, so as to be close to the water. John tramped up to the ridge behind the meadow, seeing there what Mrs. Waverly had discovered: that they were indeed on an island, perhaps ten miles long and five or six across at its widest point, nowhere of very great elevation.

From even the modest height of the ridge, however, it was possible to spot the rock that had slain the *Harmony*, offshore on the island's windward side. John could make out what he thought might be wreckage and bodies, littering the beach there.

"More dead men," said Sejanus, who had walked up after him. "Wish they'd just gone down to the bottom and stayed there."

"Aye," said John. "There was a lot of provisions on board, though. Wonder if they've floated up?"

"The flour and salt beef and all?" Sejanus rubbed his

chin. "Would you want to eat them, after they'd been in the sea?"

"We don't know how long we'll be here," said John. "You go two weeks without eating, and just see how particular you are about a little spoilt food."

Sejanus sighed. "True enough," he said.

They found a trail down to the other side of the island, and on the way spotted what had made it; for a she-goat and a pair of kids ran bleating from them. They heard answering cries from off in the brush. "Stroke of luck!" said John. "Fresh meat."

"If we can catch them," said Sejanus.

They got to the other shore and there the dead were all men they knew, including some who had been on the *Fraternity;* so they knew she must have gone down as well, but there was no sign of her. The wreck of the *Harmony,* though, was clear to see, especially once they waded out across the rock pools and looked down through the clear water and waving weed. She had broken her keel and her whole stern lay, almost intact, just offshore; her bow lay a little further beyond.

"Tide's in," said John, studying the wreck. "We can maybe dive on her, once it goes out."

They went back up to the camp in good spirits, to find that Mrs. Waverly had built a fire, and that Mr. Tudeley had opened one of the kegs that had floated ashore and found it full of rum. So you can well imagine their spirits rose higher then; and after a dinner of whelks cooked in coconut-meat, they rigged a couple of tents of sailcloth, and sat around the fire feeling pleased with themselves.

"I must say," said Mr. Tudeley, a little thickly (for he had been helping himself to the rum with a liberal hand), "regrettable as all the death is, I rather enjoy this state of nature."

"How do you mean?" Sejanus asked him. Mr. Tudeley waved his hand at their surroundings.

"The bounty of Providence here for the taking. Food and drink, with no trouble about money or shops. No concern for one's appearance. No employers or patrons with which to be troubled."

"It must seem rather an Eden," said Mrs. Waverly.

"Oh, by no means," said Mr. Tudeley, and dipped his coconut-shell in the rum once more. "Rather more Cyclopean, you know. The law is what we please, here. Were some bully from that Dutchman to have survived, and was he to come up here and demand our rum or our goods—why, we might shoot him dead, with no constable to lay hands on us, nor any magistrate to hang us for it."

"We'd need a pistol," said John.

"Well, of course we'd need a pistol, but that's not the point, is it?" said Mr. Tudeley. "What the point is, is that here we are free to look after our own interests. And after a lifetime of looking after the interests of others, I find it refreshing, upon my soul I do. Society places so many constraints upon one."

"You like it with the shackles off, do you?" said Sejanus, amused.

"Shackles! The very word, sir, yes, the very word! Do you know, sir, I had occasion to reflect upon my whole life whilst I hung there from that hideous platform, awaiting death."

"You been doing that anyway, lately," said John.

"Yes. Well. In the storm it all resolved for me, in a moment of dreadful clarity. What had my life been but

one long round of timid, smiling, obsequious servitude?"
Mr. Tudeley belched. "A worm, sir, no more but a worm. A
slave, no less than you were." He raised his cup in a salute to
Sejanus, who did not smile.

"You don't know anything about slavery," he said.

"I know that it is not to be endured," said Mr. Tudeley.

Next day they repaired the one broken oar they'd found,
and taking it and the other John rowed the boat round to the
windward side of the island. In Port Royal there had been
an old wreck sunk outside the harbor, from Spanish days,
and penniless fellows on the beach used to go try their luck
diving on her to see what they might find. John himself had
tried it, for he was a strong swimmer with a big chest; so he
was elected as their diver now.

Sejanus and Mr. Tudeley sat in the boat and lowered a
makeshift anchor. John, stripped down to a breech-clout tied
on with rope, took up one of the rocks they'd brought out
with them, and jumped over the side with it.

Almost at once he found himself standing on the aft
deck of the *Harmony*, blinking around in the clear water.
The strong light of the sun came amber through the swaying
weeds, softened to a sort of cathedral twilight. John lugged
the stone to the companionway, remembering how he'd clung
there in the last few moments before going overboard.

He jumped down through it now. There before him was
the narrow little passage to the cabins. Most of the cargo
deck, what was left of it, was empty; but he saw a few barrels
floating up against the underside of the deck, trapped there
by their buoyancy. He let go the rock and pushed them, one

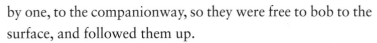

by one, to the companionway, so they were free to bob to the surface, and followed them up.

"How fare you, sir?" called Mr. Tudeley.

"Well enough," said John, when he had gulped in some air. "Nothing much but barrels down there. Might be more over t'the other half."

"I wonder, sir, whether you might fetch up my trunk?"

"What?"

"I had a change of clothes in it, you see, and some small necessary things I wished to keep."

Muttering to himself, John swam to the boat to fetch another rock; but it occurred to him that Mrs. Waverly's trunk was down there as well, to say nothing of his own. He took another deep breath and dove again, letting the rock sink him down the companionway. There he released it and pulled himself along the passage to the cabins. And there he almost yelled aloud; for he looked up into the white face of the French sharpshooter who'd helped him fire the swivel gun. The man floated face down, trapped against the underside of the aft deck. His last breath was a silver bubble in his open mouth.

Grimacing, John grabbed a fistful of the man's shirt and pulled him down, backing away with him and letting him go at the companionway. The dead man drifted through, turning slowly as he went. The bubble escaped from his mouth and fled upward like a fish. John followed, looking around on the deck to see what else he might grab on this trip, and spotted the swivel gun on the broken rail. He swam over and wrenched at it until it came loose, rail and all. Cradling it in his arms, he pushed off against the deck and broke the surface.

"Got this," he gasped, manhandling it over the side into the boat.

"What use is that, may I ask?" said Mr. Tudeley, scowling at it through sweat-fogged spectacles.

"You never know. She's a sweet little gun, and company may come to call," said John, wiping his face with one hand.

He dove four more times before he had to stop; it took a dive each to fetch up their trunks, and on the last he spotted two cutlasses and a pistol lying up against the bulkhead. Too weary to climb into the boat (which was now full of salvage in any case) John simply clung to the stern and rode it back as Sejanus rowed them ashore.

The first thing he did, after he staggered dripping ashore, was haul out Mrs. Waverly's trunk and open it. Tilting it, he spilled out gowns and shoes and toilet things, all soaked. He sorted through them hastily to see if he could find Tom Blackstone's letter. Letter there was none, even in the little inlaid box that had been tucked under the bottom layer of her garments. John opened it and found only the earrings Captain Reynald had given her, with some hairpins and a few trinkets he suspected she'd stolen.

He closed the box and became aware that Sejanus and Mr. Tudeley were watching him. "Just wanted to be certain sure she wasn't robbed," he said.

"If you say so," said Sejanus, raising one eyebrow.

They buried more bodies before they started back—with somewhat less ceremony, funerals being impractical when corpses were becoming so commonplace. Mrs. Waverly rose from where she had been tending the fire, and smiled to see what John carried.

"My trunk!" she exclaimed. "Why, Mr. James, how dear,

how *thoughtful* of you!" She ran to him and stood on tiptoe, pulling him down for a kiss.

"It was a pleasure, ma'am," said John. In his best bluff and honest manner, he added: "Mind, we had to open it to drain the water out, and your things fell out too, so they're a bit disordered. But I put everything back in."

"You have my eternal gratitude," said Mrs. Waverly. "What luck that we have fresh water! I can launder everything tomorrow. Do let me launder your shirts and stockings as well, Mr. James."

"I have shirts and stockings too," volunteered Mr. Tudeley, but she didn't seem to hear him.

She made on a great deal over John that evening, serving him his coconut and whelks first, mixing him a treat of rum and coconut-water, and nestling up beside him when they sat by the fire afterward.

The conversation ran on what they ought to look for next in the diving, whether the carpenter's chest or the navigation gear, and from thence it proceeded to where they would go once they'd built their pinnace.

"Mind you, we need to know whereabouts we are, first," said John. "If we can find the charts and they ain't too spoilt, we can chart a course. Can't just sail off into the blue."

"How very wise, Mr. James," said Mrs. Waverly, sliding her arm through his. He looked at her sidelong. "You and I, of course, ought to proceed to Leauchaud. Once we have resolved those matters concerning my poor husband's estate, we might consider anything! Should you care to travel? Have you ever been to Paris?"

"I was thinking of settling down in Port Royal," said John, but the high-colored image of going to Paris with Mrs.

Waverly dazzled him, as it had been meant to do. To clear his head of images of Mrs. Waverly in a lace peignoir, he said: "What'll you do, Mr. Tudeley? Go on to Barbados?"

"That's a question, indeed, sir," said Mr. Tudeley, staring into the fire. "You know...I don't believe I shall. I ought to send to Arabella to let her know I'm well, of course. But, in a way, this whole mischance has been a blessing in disguise. A veil has dropped from my eyes, sir. I have perceived now that, life being so miserably brief and tenuous, one ought to spend it in what enjoyment one can, don't you think? And the essentials of life are so much more easily come by in a place less constrained by Society.

"I rather liked Tortuga. It was a jolly place, quite free and easy! I think perhaps I may settle at Tortuga. Yes." Mr. Tudeley helped himself to a little more rum. He looked across the fire at Sejanus. "What of you, sir? Shall you go back to Africa?"

Sejanus shook his head. "How can I go back to a place where I've never been?" he said, adding another bit of driftwood to the fire. "No. What would I do there? No one would speak English, and I know only a few words of the talk. Mud houses and cattle pens and strangers...what's that to me? Get myself taken up again as a slave, most likely.

"Then again...no sense going back to Boston. Or Virginia. Laws change too fast. I went to sea because I heard there are no nations among sailors. I heard that on a ship, a man's as good as the work he can do. I was sadly misinformed...Wasn't true under Captain Sharp, no, sir. I was only one inch higher than a slave, to him. But it was true under Reynald. First time I was ever around white men who treated me like one of them. Pity, Reynald dying...maybe I'll

Or Else My Lady Keeps the Key

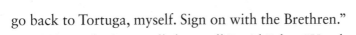

go back to Tortuga, myself. Sign on with the Brethren."

"Piracy don't pay all that well," said John. "You know, there's places inland where slaves go when they escape. Lots of 'em live back in the caves and such. Supposed to be whole villages, hiding up in the mountains on Hispaniola. D'you ever think of going to live with them?"

"But I'm not an escaped slave," said Sejanus. "I was manumitted free and clear. I'm not going to run and hide from anyone."

"You'll have to, if you're a pirate," said John. "Except for the other Brethren, every man's hand will be against you."

"Every man's hand is already against me," said Sejanus, with a humorless chuckle. "But at least it won't be just because of the color of my skin, if I'm looting treasure and burning galleons."

THIRTEEN:

Domestic Economy

THEY ROWED OUT FARTHER next day to the bow of the *Harmony*. Here the water was deeper, the diving harder, but it was worth it; for here John brought up what proved to be the carpenter's chest at last, as well as a few barrels of salt beef.

And here he spotted one-pound shot scattered across the sea floor like windfall apples under a tree, and busied himself collecting as many as he could each dive, gathering them into a sack he'd made from an old coat sleeve tied off at one end. The coat's owner was beyond caring, but they had buried him a little deeper, just in case, and muttered a few prayers over him to make up for it.

John was crouched over, scooping up a few last shot on his fifth dive, when he heard a thundering knocking from above, as though they in the boat were beating on the gunwales. Which, as it turned out, was just what they were doing, trying frantically to get his attention.

He turned to look upward and was hit in the shoulder

by a gray shape that struck him hard, flowing smoothly past. He turned, peering through his floating hair, and saw a reef shark turning to come back at him. Straight at his face it came, a big dead-eyed bugger like a battering ram. John, terrified, swung his fistful of shot and hit it square on the nose. Its forward momentum was halted; a sort of caul veiled its eyes, as though it was squinting. As it paused in front of him John grabbed its head, with his thumbs through the gills on either side, and rammed his forehead into its nose.

The shark shook violently. John let go, pushing off from the bottom. Sejanus was already reaching down for him, and grabbed him under the arms as he broke the surface. He hauled him half into the boat. John clutched at the thwarts and writhed forward, trying to lift his lower body out of the water, but felt something hit his calf and then sharp pain there. He bellowed in fear. Sejanus grabbed hold of the back of his breech-clout and hauled so hard it came off, but did succeed in getting John the rest of the way into the boat.

John, still screaming, heard Mr. Tudeley grunting with effort as he struck at something with an oar. Then the oar was hitting John across the back of his legs too, which hurt rather more than the other pain, and he heard Sejanus laughing. John turned in outrage and saw Mr. Tudeley clubbing a dogfish that had come into the boat with its teeth sunk in John's calf. It lay now detached in the bottom of the boat, stunned, and John was bleeding like a stuck pig from a circular wound in his leg.

Sejanus was still laughing so hard he couldn't speak, but he grabbed the oar from Mr. Tudeley and rowed them ashore as quickly as he could. It wasn't until he ran them aground that he was able to catch his breath enough to say: "Bind up his leg with the breech-clout, Winty! You've killed us a nice fish for dinner, too. White men make good bait, I guess, eh?"

They went back up the trail to the other side of the island. Mr. Tudeley ran ahead to the camp, to fetch John back a pair of breeches, while John limped along leaning on Sejanus. He felt dizzy and faint.

"Could have been worse," said Sejanus. "Could have been the big one got your leg. You don't go back in the water until your leg heals up, eh? Maybe Winty and I will try our luck. Maybe out on the Dutchman's wreck. She had a big fine stern cabin; daresay there's charts and sextants and such in there. Come on, don't you go swooning. Talk to me! How do we build a pinnace? You ever built a boat before?"

"No," said John. "I just reckoned we'd make it like the longboat. Only bigger."

"Use the longboat as a pattern? That's good. That'll work. Collect the busted bits of wreck that's washed ashore, eh? Some fine big planks washed up. Come on, keep walking, not much farther now. I see the camp. Oh, lord—" Sejanus began laughing again, and John gave a strangled cry of horror.

Mrs. Waverly, clad only in a shift, was running to meet them, closely pursued by Mr. Tudeley, who was waving his hands and protesting "But ma'am—but, ma'am!" Sejanus, with great presence of mind, snatched off his scarf and screened John's privates with it.

"You was supposed to bring my breeches," John shouted at Mr. Tudeley.

"It's not my fault! She's *washed* everything," protested Mr. Tudeley.

"Oh, my poor Mr. James!" Mrs. Waverly fell to her knees beside John. She loosed the breech clout to examine his wound and it promptly gushed forth blood again. "Oh, my dear! This must be sewn up!"

John tried to explain that all he needed was a tighter bandage and a good-lie down and some rum, but somehow he came over all strange. The next thing he knew, he was lying on his face in camp and hearing Mrs. Waverly saying, "Hold his hands, for this will sting." He yelled and started up when she splashed rum in the wound, and only Sejanus holding him down (and the consciousness that he was still naked under a bit of sailcloth) kept him from jumping to his feet. He put his head down and swore.

"Please don't use that sort of language, Mr. James," said Mrs. Waverly, threading a needle. "It ill becomes you."

"I'm sorry, ma'am," said John, and gritted his teeth as she stitched him up.

He was given a big shellful of coconut water and rum afterward, and told to lie quiet. He was content enough to do this, sipping his rum and watching Mrs. Waverly move about the camp. Her shift was of rather fine material and gave the imagination a lot to work with. It seemed to unnerve Mr. Tudeley, who blushed and stammered, and stared when he didn't think she noticed.

The whole camp had a domestic appearance now, with fresh-laundered laundry spread out on bushes to dry in the sun, for all the world like washing-day in the fields by Hackney Brook. Sejanus went back and fetched up the dogfish, which he gutted and cleaned. Mrs. Waverly cut it into steaks and grilled them over the coals. Later she knelt by John and fed him choice bits with her fingers, smiling and chatting on inconsequential matters with such grace and elegance, she might have been at Court.

"Now, dear Mr. James, I hope you'll indulge me by drinking a little more coconut water," she said at last, wiping her hands.

"Yes, ma'am," said John. "I'm sorry about the indecency, ma'am."

She laughed gaily. "Why, Mr. James, a gentleman in his natural state is not indecent if there is no lewd purpose to his undress. In any case, we are presently far from Society and its constraints, as Mr. Tudeley pointed out." She patted his shoulder, and perhaps her hand lingered a moment too long on his bare skin. "Nor are you an ill-favored man."

"Very kind of you to say so, I'm sure," he said, trying not to notice that he could see her nipples through the gauzy fabric of her shift.

John might have died and gone to Fiddler's Green, so pleasant his next couple of days were; for he had nothing to do but lie in the shade in his shirt, and sip coconut water while Sejanus and Mr. Tudeley worked at collecting planks from the wreckage scattered on both sides of the island. They had a go at diving on the Dutchman's wreck themselves, from which they did manage to recover some navigational gear and sodden charts, before another reef shark came cruising to see what they were doing.

Mrs. Waverly found that going about in her shift was altogether so comfortable and convenient, in the intemperate heat, that she declined to wear anything else. John fashioned himself a crutch to hobble about with for necessary purposes, but mostly he lay still as he had been bid, with his bandaged leg propped up on a roll of sailcloth. He watched Mrs. Waverly's bare ankles twinkling about, and observed keenly as she bent over to stir fish-broth simmering in the pot they had salvaged, or crouched to rub fish oil into the leather of her shoes. His leg hurt a bit, and itched powerfully as the wound began to heal, but she treated him as tenderly as though he were at death's door. John was altogether a happy man.

Mr. Tudeley, on the other hand, was quite flustered. The first day or so he avoided looking at Mrs. Waverly at all, averting his eyes from her whenever possible.

The second day, however, he dispensed with his own shirt, announcing that Society might require a man to be miserable in the heat, but he was damned if he was going to sweat in the sun like a roasting ham. He burned quite painfully red as a consequence.

He took to swaggering, too.

"Well, here's the damned salt beef," he announced, setting down a keg he had hauled up from the beach. "I declare, gentlemen, I am developing a prodigious appetite for meat. It must be the free air; for in Spanish Town I was so dyspeptic, I could scarcely stomach dry biscuit without a glass of wormwood cordial first. I find my natural appetite wonderfully revived. Perhaps you'd be good enough to cook us a dish of stewed beef, ma'am?"

"That's not beef," said Sejanus. "That's one of the powder kegs."

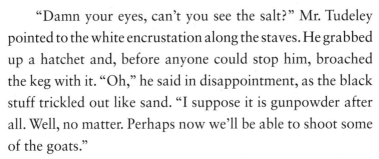

"Damn your eyes, can't you see the salt?" Mr. Tudeley pointed to the white encrustation along the staves. He grabbed up a hatchet and, before anyone could stop him, broached the keg with it. "Oh," he said in disappointment, as the black stuff trickled out like sand. "I suppose it is gunpowder after all. Well, no matter. Perhaps now we'll be able to shoot some of the goats."

"I don't think so," said Mrs. Waverly, coming to look into the keg. She frowned. "What you took for salt is *saltpeter*, Mr. Tudeley. It has leached out in the seawater and spoilt the powder."

"Damn," said John, and parenthetically added "Excuse me, ma'am. Are they all like that? And there I went to all the trouble of fetching up that swivel gun."

"It is of no consequence," said Mrs. Waverly, looking serene. "I shall simply prepare more saltpeter."

As one man, they stared at her. "Where'd you learn to do that?" said John.

"In my travels with my late husband," she said, and smiled, and declined to explain further.

It turned out that if Mr. Tudeley and Sejanus took the boat out to a certain rock just offshore, that was white as snow with birdshite and hot as a griddle, and spent a hellish hour or so chipping away enough of it to fill a bucket, half the work was done. John lay back in the shade, watching them complacently.

"Will you have a little more rum, Mr. James?" Mrs. Waverly inquired, bending down to him.

"Why, yes, ma'am, that's mighty kind of you," said John. She presented him with a coconut-shell full and settled down by him, taking care that her thigh pressed against his own. But she sat otherwise upright and proper, with her hands folded in her lap, gazing out at Sejanus and Mr. Tudeley as they worked.

"I must commend you on your admirable restraint, Mr. James," she said. "In all the while we have been here, you have not attempted anything in the least improper. This despite the necessity of a state of dress that would be deemed immodest in London, and the prodigious quantities of rum you have been obliged to imbibe for medicinal reasons."

John considered her narrowly, wondering what she might be about. He had a swallow of rum and thought carefully before he replied.

"Well, ma'am, it's not that I ain't been tempted. You're a beauty, by thunder; but there's such a thing as loyalty to friends, ain't there? You was with my shipmate Tom. He was gently born and all; why, he knew princes. And here's me, a bricklayer's apprentice from Hackney. I ain't such a fool as to suppose I could supplant the likes of him."

"Not *supplant*," said Mrs. Waverly, with a sigh. "None shall ever replace dear Tom in my affections. But he is—oh, how can I pronounce the hated word?—dead. And you and I have been through a great deal together, Mr. James. I do hope that, when my period of mourning is concluded, you will not allow delicacy to prevent you from making so bold as to consider me more than your friend." And she placed her hand on his leg, pretty close to Wapping Dock and Walls.

John had a stiff drink of rum while he tried to reason through the exact meaning of her words.

"Well," he said cautiously. "We'll see, I expect. Well! H'm. So. Was there a Mr. Waverly, then?"

"Briefly," she said. "And then I met a gallant cavalier. Poor Tom had been improvident with his inheritance; he was therefore obliged to live by his bravery and his wits, and I with him."

"Where'd you learn to make saltpeter, really?"

"Flanders," Mrs. Waverly replied, with a slight shrug. "We were besieged. One made do with what one could improvise. But what of you, dear Mr. James? Had you a wife or sweetheart in London?"

"No—oo," said John, "At least, no wife. There were girls and all. None that'll be missing me." He thought briefly of the girl he had lost in Panama, and winced.

"There is no claim on your heart then?" Mrs. Waverly leaned back and lay down beside him, smiling into his eyes.

"Er," said John. "No, ma'am."

"I am glad to hear it," said Mrs. Waverly, and kissed him, slowly. She pressed him back and he yielded to her push, feeling his heart pounding. He groped to pull his shirt down in front, but her hand was somehow there in the way, and everything was going along splendidly when he raised his eyes and saw a black face laughing at him from the branches above. A young girl, very pretty, with long black ringlets trailing down and wicked mischief in her eyes. She wore a pink cotton gown. John saw her clear as he saw Mrs. Waverly, and he was seeing Mrs. Waverly close and clear indeed.

His eyes widened and he caught his breath, just as Mrs. Waverly sat up abruptly.

"Oh, dear," she said, in tones of real irritation. "The others have returned."

John leaned up on his elbow and saw Sejanus and Mr. Tudeley had quitted the rock and were just now stepping ashore, bearing their malodorous prize. He looked up into the branches again, but the young girl had vanished.

"How tedious," muttered Mrs. Waverly. Yet she received the bucketful when Mr. Tudeley brought it up to camp, smiling graciously as though it contained the first strawberries of the season, and promptly carried it off to distill it with wood ash.

"And how is the brave hero?" Sejanus inquired, selecting a couple of coconuts from the pile they had gathered.

"Well enough," said John crossly.

"Poor hero. Did we interrupt your courting?" Sejanus drew his cutlass and sliced away the top of one coconut, as easily as opening a jar. He tossed it to Mr. Tudeley, who had collapsed gasping in the shade, and opened the other for himself.

"No," said John. "And none of your business anyhow, whatever we was doing."

"Suit yourself," said Sejanus. He had a long drink of coconut water.

"But that little black miss that was so taken with you at Tortuga was hanging about," said John, with a spiteful grin as Sejanus choked.

"What do you mean?" he inquired, when he had wiped coconut water from his nose and chin.

John pointed into the tree and told him. Sejanus glanced up into the branches. His eyes narrowed.

"Nothing there now," he said. "Nothing at all. That's how it is with *imaginary* things. Like those old loas, back in Africa. People imagined them up, you see? But this isn't Africa, there's nobody to make them real here. And so they have no power here. Shadows and tricks of the light, that's all they are. And that's all they'll stay."

There came a sudden clatter of hooves on the ridge above them. To their amazement, a goat came running straight through camp. Mr. Tudeley flung himself sideways and grabbed for it, managing to catch hold of a hind leg. It fell, bleating and struggling.

"What extraordinary luck!" he gasped. "Kill it, sir, kill it!"

Before he quite knew what he was doing, Sejanus's cutlass flashed in the air. The goat's head flew off in a burst of blood and rolled in the sand; the blood-jet hissed in the coals of the fire. The goat continued twitching and kicking a moment longer.

"Oh, well done, sir!" said Mr. Tudeley.

"Roast goat for dinner!" said John, applauding. And neither of them could understand why Sejanus flung down the cutlass with a grimace of disgust, and stormed off to walk the beach by himself.

FOURTEEN:

Fables

IT HAD BEEN A young goat, and roasted up well, with a lot of dripping that they caught carefully in a coconut shell; not for eating, but to grease up the swivel gun and the pistol. They celebrated the fresh meat with abundant rum, and grew very merry about the fire; all except Sejanus, who seemed sullen and out of sorts.

"I declare, sir," said Mr. Tudeley, "This is most unlike you. Be of good cheer! The night is fine, the company excellent. Perhaps someone knows a diverting song or story? What of you, Mr. James? Will you not entertain us with some sort of sailor lore?"

John looked up, blinking sleepily. He had taken on board as much supper as he could hold, and would have liked nothing better than to nod off there by the fire. But he sat upright and rubbed his whiskery chin.

"Well," he said. "Sailor lore. Don't know any sailor lore, to speak of. But I know a story, I guess.

"There was this boy named Dick, see. And he was real

poor. Youngest of three and his oldest brother got the farm, and his sister got the money laid by to be her dowry, and so all that was left to him when the will was read was the cat.

"So he has to go out into the world to seek his fortune. And the cat says, 'What are you looking so downcast for?'

"And Dick's surprised and all, because a cat can't talk, can it? So he says to the cat, he says, 'I didn't know you could talk, Puss.' And Puss says, 'Ah, well, I can do a lot more than talk. I'm a lucky cat, I am. Just you make me a nice pair of boots to wear, and a gentleman's hat, and make sure I always have enough cream and fish for my dinner, and I'll fetch you anything you want.'"

"And the fool gave him the boots and hat, didn't he?" said Sejanus.

"Aye," said John. "So, the cat eats the fish, and drinks up the cream, and puts on the hat and boots, and stands up like a little man. 'Come on, master,' he says, 'The first thing we got to do is find a ship.' So they go somewhere, Portsmouth or Bristol or Dover maybe, and they ship out on a vessel bound for Araby. And pretty soon the other sailors is jealous, because Dick's got this talking cat, see? And they start to talk amongst themselves about how it ain't natural, and they ought to pitch both Dick and the cat overboard on account of Dick being a wizard.

"But the cat gets to hear about it, on account of he's always sneaking about as cats do, and he goes and digs out this almanac he pinched from a bookseller's stall afore they left land, and he reads up on the weather that's to come, and next day he stands in the waist of the ship and starts to prophesy how the weather's going to be. Captain hears him from the quarterdeck and says, 'What the hell are you?'

"The cat jumps up on the quarterdeck and doffs his hat all respectful and says, 'If you please, sir, I'm a lucky weather-predicting cat, and I belong to Dick Whittington.' Captain likes cats, and he thinks it's real pretty the cat's got on a little hat and boots. 'Well, ain't you the sweety-weetiest thing!' quoth he. 'You shall be my own cat now, and predict the weather for me, and that way I'll always have smooth sailing.'

"But Puss says, 'Oh, no, dear Captain, I'm a loyal cat, and I couldn't possibly leave my own dear master Dick unless you was to give him your golden sword and your big pistol, and your plumy hat besides.' So the captain grumbles a bit but he gives Dick his golden sword and his big pistol and his plumy hat, see?

"And then Puss goes to live in the Captain's cabin and gets the best fish on a golden plate, and sleeps on a goosedown cushion, and never has to turn out in foul weather like the poor sailors do."

"Typical," said Sejanus.

"I expect Dick felt himself ill-used," said Mrs. Waverly.

"Well, you have to wait and see how it turns out," said John. "See, all the while the cat's living in the captain's cabin, he's studying on the captain's charts. And at night he creeps down into the ship and steals stores, and wraps them up in canvas and hides 'em in the boat. Then he goes into Dick's sea chest, and he takes out the golden sword and the big pistol and the plumy hat and he hides them in the boat too. Pretty soon he's ready, and he says, 'Captain dear, I have a secret to tell you. There's an island of pure gold not far away, and I can take you there; but you'll have to let me do the steering, because only I know the course.'

"Captain says, 'Why then, you take the tiller, Puss; just you get us there as fast as you can!'

"So Puss takes the tiller, and stays there all day and into the dark of night. And just as the moon sets, he runs them hard on a rock, and in the shock and the crash he jumps up and blows all the lamps out. So when everyone comes running up on deck it's black as pitch, and no man knows what's what.

"But Puss can see in the dark, you know, and he jumps on Dick's shoulder and says 'Now, master, just you get into the boat and cast off sharp.' Which Dick does. Puss bends to the oars and rows them away quick from the wreck, which has been holed pretty bad, and the men work like devils to get her off the rock at high tide, but when she works free, it turns out the hole's bigger than it looked; she fills and goes down with all hands."

"What a dreadful little creature!" said Mr. Tudeley.

"It's a *cat*," said John. "What d'you expect? So then, Puss rows them up on the shore, where there's a big heathen city. And Puss says, 'Quick now, bind on the golden sword, and stick the big pistol in your belt, and put the plumy hat on your head." So Dick does, and then the heathen folk all come out of their palaces to stare at Dick and his cat. And Puss talks to them, because he can talk their yowly foreign talk, and what he tells them is, his master's the King of England, who's been in a shipwreck and landed on their shores.

"Well, they ain't never seen the like, neither of Dick nor his cat, so they take him to the Grand Turk. And on the way to the Grand Turk's palace Puss is looking all around, because there's rats running in and out of the shops, and there's rats in the eating-houses stealing food off peoples'

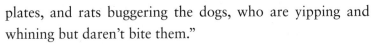
plates, and rats buggering the dogs, who are yipping and whining but daren't bite them."

"Mr. James!"

"I mean—I mean—hoping you'll excuse me, ma'am. Strike that last bit. So anyhow they go to the Grand Turk. The Grand Turk, he says, 'By the powers, what're you?" And Puss falls down flat and knocks his head on the Grand Turk's shoe three times, and says, "Oh Grand Turk, may I introduce my master, the King of England? Hoping you'll treat a fellow prince friendly-like, as his great grand ship with golden masts and silver spars and silken sails was most unfortunate lost at sea, and only we two escaped. He'd like to know if you can loan him the borrow of a ship to get home.'

"The Grand Turk looks them over and he's seen men aplenty, but never seen no cat afore, in boots or out of 'em. He says, 'Tell my fellow prince I'm sorry to say it, but we've fallen on hard times here on account of all these rats, and I can't spare a ship nor any men to crew her.'

"Well! Puss grins, like a cat will, and says 'I can fix your rats, oh Grand Turk. Just you make my master the King comfortable, and I'll go out and have a word with 'em for you, shall I?'

"And he goes out and grins at the rats and says, 'Right, my lads, you're for it.' And he sets about killing, and the ones as isn't murdered straight away runs off so far they're never seen again. He bites the heads off a round dozen or so and lugs 'em in by the whiskers, and says: 'I reckon this lot won't be troubling you any more, oh Grand Turk.'

"The Grand Turk's mighty pleased at that, and says: 'My fine fellow, are there other creatures like you in

England?' Puss bows low and he says, 'Why, yes, there are a few of us. We only work for the very finest lords and ladies, though.'

"Grand Turk says, 'How much would one of your lords or ladies ask, to sell such wonderful rat-killers?'

"Puss, he says 'Oh, I don't know if they'd sell one of us for less than a dozen chests of treasure. But, of course, you wouldn't want just one; you'd want a gentlemen cat and a lady cat too, you see? And that way you'd soon be raising your own. So I would say twenty-five chests of treasure, on account of the ladies always cost more.'

"Grand Turk says, 'Then I will load my best galley with presents for your King of England, and send him home in rare fashion. And I will put in twenty-five chests of treasure too, and when he gets back, he will surely send me a pair of rat-killers.'

"Puss bows low and says, 'To be sure, Mr. Grand Turk, that he will.'

"So it was done. And Dick Whittington got home with his fortune made, and the heathen sailors was all pressed by the Navy so they couldn't go back and tell no tales. And Puss lived like a Grand Turk himself the rest of his days, with all the cream he could drink, and all the fish he could eat."

"Did you learn that story at your mother's knee?" demanded Mr. Tudeley, scandalized.

"Some of it," said John. "I made up bits where I didn't remember. It's only a fairy-story anyhow."

"It had no morally instructive value whatever, I am afraid," said Mrs. Waverly, with a solemn face.

"Chah! Like enough the cat would get his hat and boots, and sweet cream the rest of his days," said Sejanus, with a sneer. He dipped himself another coconut-shellful of rum, and drank. "But I doubt he'd do anything for the boy in return. I'd say the boy worked to the end of *his* days keeping the cat happy."

"Like enough," said John, with a chuckle.

"You never want to give them what they ask for," muttered Sejanus, taking another drink. "Because, see, then you believe in them. And that's like chains on your reason. Good blacksmith can take shackles off your legs, but nobody can take off the other kind. And you put them on yourself. That's the worst of it."

"I beg your pardon?" said Mr. Tudeley.

"I am a free man," said Sejanus, raising his voice. "And I intend to stay that way, you hear?"

"Maybe you had enough rum for tonight, mate," said John, right before Mrs. Waverly screamed.

John sat bolt upright and almost screamed himself. Out at the edge of the firelight, just beyond the little palisado fence they had put up, stood a dead man.

It was the black they had found staring up from the rock pool, the one they had buried a good six feet down on the beach. He was dripping wet, with sand in his hair. He did not stare empty-eyed now; he gazed straight at Sejanus, looking sullen and resentful.

Sejanus turned and saw him, and leaped to his feet, spilling his rum. The dead man raised his arm and held out his hand, like someone asking for payment.

Sejanus turned his back. "No!" he said fiercely. "Don't look at him, don't think about him. You!" He grabbed Mr. Tudeley, who was staring at the dead man with his eyes standing out of his head. "Look at me! We're reasoning

men, aren't we? No damn superstitions. You don't see any-thing there!"

"But—but, sir, I must say I do—" said Mr. Tudeley, in a kind of gobbling squawk.

"No, you don't!" Sejanus lifted him bodily and turned him toward the fire. "Nobody does! Look at the fire instead. You, too!" he added to Mrs. Waverly and John. "There's no haunts. Nothing there in the dark. Close your eyes if you're scared. Sing!'

He smacked the side of John's head and John, keeping his eyes resolutely on the fire, began: *"Taking his beer with old Anacharsis…"*

They sang it three times through, with Mrs. Waverly joining in as well, though her voice trembled and she gripped John's hand fair to break his fingers.

When they fell silent at last, John dared to look up at the palisadoes and saw nothing there. Sejanus grabbed a burning branch from the fire and scrambled to his feet. He went to the palisadoes and stared out at the night, holding the torch high.

"There is *nothing* there!" he shouted, and flung the branch. And nothing answered him; there was only the sound of the wind in the palm trees, and the soft boom and crash of the surf.

FIFTEEN:

Visitors

BY THE BROAD LIGHT of day it seemed best to pretend nothing strange had ever happened, though John got up early and went limping out on his crutch to look at the sand on the other side of the palisadoes. There were no footsteps there, nor any ghastly trail leading up from the black's burying-place. A couple more corpses from the wreck had washed up on the shore in the night, to be sure, and the sharks had been at them, so John took an oar and went down on his knees to dig graves for them. He was getting so used to dead men by now, though, he might have been a householder in London sweeping down his front step.

With John able to totter about, they set to building the pinnace. Sejanus seemed to want to throw himself into hard work, and his momentum carried the others along. They labored in the sun, sweating to drag timbers from the wreck;

it was a long weary business sawing a keel from the biggest beam, and they were obliged to dive the wrecks again to get enough hull-planking, though the sharks came eagerly to see what they were doing.

In the end they made a sort of grenade with some of the gunpowder in a coconut-shell. They set it smoldering and shut it quick in a weighted barrel, and dropped it over the side of the boat above the wreck, rowing away like hell. Mrs. Waverly's saltpeter proved to work admirably; there was a belch of white water and the sea above the wreck foamed like a kettle on the boil. A great deal of planking floated ashore after that.

Unfortunately more dead men washed up too, pretty far gone now, disturbed by the concussion. They went into one mass grave, pitched in without ceremony, nothing more than nuisances now.

The living changed too. The men shaved at intervals, to keep their faces cooler, but the work stained and the sun bleached what they wore, and nobody bothered with stockings or shoes. Mr. Tudeley plaited himself a straw hat from palm fronds, which gave him a rakish look. Mrs. Waverly was very particular about washing and keeping her hair combed out fine, but she did persist in wearing nothing but a shift, and nothing under it as far as anyone could tell. And though she continued affectionate with John, she kept a prim distance from him by night, sleeping in her own little bower rigged up under a canvas sunshade.

John was too weary, after a day of hard work, to press for more. His restraint seemed to embolden Mr. Tudeley, who one day announced he was just going for a coconut.

"Either of you fellows care for one? I've a damned perishing thirst." he said, elaborately casual.

Sejanus, busy planing a length of broken plank into a rudder for the pinnace, merely grunted his refusal. "Aye, thank'ee," said John, who was hobbling back and forth in the sun like a donkey, dragging planks and beams from their lumber pile.

They worked on a while. At last John stopped, wiped his face on his sleeve and glared at the little heap of pegs Mr. Tudeley had been set to whittle.

"Where's he got to, anyhow?"

"I reckon it's all the fresh air," said Sejanus cryptically, as he worked.

"What's that?"

"Didn't you notice? He's been using the word *damn* all morning. Damn this, damn that, damn hot sun, damn wet wood. Did a lot of talking about damned Society and its damned restraints. Must be feeling powerful manly today."

"Oh."

"Well, I'd like my God-damned coconut," said John. Sejanus snickered.

"I reckon he would too."

"I'll go get it myself, then," said John, and started up the sand dune. As he came limping over the top he met Mr. Tudeley staggering back. Mr. Tudeley's spectacles hung under his chin; one lens had been broken, and he had a split lip.

"Where's my coconut? And what happened to you?" John demanded.

"Oh! I just thought I'd...see if there were fresher coconuts on the tree, you know, and I made to climb one, and, er, fell," said Mr. Tudeley, pulling his straw hat down in

a vain attempt to shade his face. He had lost another tooth, too. "Terribly sorry."

He wobbled on past John, who watched him go and then hastened back to camp. There he found Mrs. Waverly apparently serene and untroubled, though her color was a little high. She was weaving strips of rags into cord to make slow-match, the very picture of a thrifty housewife.

"Is all well?" John asked. She looked up at him and smiled.

"Why, of course, Mr. James. What do you lack?"

"I was only thirsty, is all."

"Ah!" She rose and, taking a cutlass, neatly whacked the top from one of the coconuts in their makeshift larder. "Allow me." She presented John with the coconut. He drank from it, thanked her, and went back to work.

As he stood looking down at the beach, John saw a line of cloud advancing over the sea, far off to the east, the same dirty coppery color as he'd noticed the morning of the storm. "Bugger," he muttered, and hurried down to the others. Sejanus had paused work to pick the broken glass out of Mr. Tudeley's spectacles. As John approached he was tying a loop through the empty half of the frame.

"There you are," he said, fastening it through Mr. Tudeley's buttonhole. "It'll dangle there and you can just hold it up to your eye when you want to look at something close."

"Not that I waste much time reading nowadays," said Mr. Tudeley, with a sigh.

"Look out there," said John, pointing at the horizon. They looked.

"Oh, hell," said Sejanus.

They spent the rest of the afternoon dragging everything they had salvaged up from the beach, and the half-finished pinnace and the boat too, as close to the center of the island as they could haul them. The clouds advanced smoothly, relentlessly, and the heat came with them. John thanked God he was safe on dry land this time.

They battened down, stowing the powderkegs under several thicknesses of canvas, and rigged a shelter with barrels and the overturned boat, for when the rain came; and yet, as the hours went by and the skittering hot wind fanned their faces, no rain fell. The sea rose and began to break on the reef with a sound like cannon fire.

"Maybe it'll miss us," said John, at sunset, looking at the red sky in the west. Sejanus shrugged.

They ate hastily of a kind of stew of salt beef and coconut water, and sat around the fire watching as night fell. All to the east and north there were flashes of lightning but an eerie lack of thunder. The wind dropped off suddenly. John, looking up at the black starless sky, felt he might as well have been in a room indoors.

"I wish it would break," said Mr. Tudeley, mopping his forehead. "The air's stifling."

Mrs. Waverly, who had risen to open a coconut for herself (she being disinclined to drink rum like the others) cried out suddenly. "Oh, the sea!"

The others jumped to their feet. Looking out over the palisadoes they could see the waves breaking in green fire. "Great God!" cried Mr. Tudeley.

"That's just, what d'you call it, that's just a red tide," said John. "Phosphorescence."

"What makes it?" demanded Sejanus. John shrugged.

"Seen it in a ship's wake plenty of times," he said. "Maybe it's something rotten in the water, same as tree stumps when they shine in the dark. Nothing to be scared of."

"Do you think it's all the drowned men?" asked Mrs. Waverly in a shaky voice.

"Suppose so," said John.

A flash of lightning came then, a flare of violet fire that ran across the sky. A long forked chain stabbed down into the sea; John could imagine the water boiling to steam where it struck, and cooked fish floating to the surface from five fathoms below.

"Storm's getting closer," said Sejanus. "Maybe we'd best—"

Another flash came, so close the branched lightning looked thick as a man's arm, white-hot as the sun's heart, with a shattering boom of thunder. John could have sworn he felt its heat scorching his face. For a second he was blind, but for the afterimage dancing in his eyes. His heart contracted with the fear that he had just seen something out at sea, briefly illuminated in the flash. Had there been masts and spars? Was some other luckless mariner out there in the night?

"Did anyone see—" began Mrs. Waverly, before the next flash came. There was a noise like a bomb rolling across the floor of heaven and then it exploded, with a roar that knocked them down. John found himself groveling in the sand at the base of the palisadoes, feeling with his fingers to be certain his eyes hadn't been burned out of his head.

"Oh, no, no, no—" Mrs. Waverly moaned. John struggled to his feet, using his crutch, and she seized his arm. "Why would anyone go to sea—"

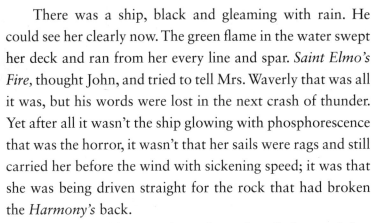

There was a ship, black and gleaming with rain. He could see her clearly now. The green flame in the water swept her deck and ran from her every line and spar. *Saint Elmo's Fire*, thought John, and tried to tell Mrs. Waverly that was all it was, but his words were lost in the next crash of thunder. Yet after all it wasn't the ship glowing with phosphorescence that was the horror, it wasn't that her sails were rags and still carried her before the wind with sickening speed; it was that she was being driven straight for the rock that had broken the *Harmony's* back.

John opened his mouth to shout, for all the good that would have done. But he made no sound; and neither did the ship, when she struck. He saw it all, he saw her strike and slew around just as the *Harmony* had done, he saw her heeling over, with her mainmast sprung and toppling from the impact. He fancied he saw the little black wet figures staggering about on her slanting deck, before the next terrible flash came and left him blinking at floating spots.

There wasn't a sound. Not even thunder. He rubbed his eyes and looked, and saw that the ship was gone. The sea beat to a glowing green mist on the rock, but there was nothing where the wreck had been a moment before.

"Where'd she go?" he cried hoarsely. His voice sounded strange and muffled in his ears. He turned to stare at the others. Mr. Tudeley and Mrs. Waverly looked on, their faces set, drained of all color. Sejanus watched stonily, with inexplicable anger.

John turned to stare at the rock again, its black spire lit by quick hectic flashes. He heard a ringing now, like a ship's bell, tolling out through the storm. He heard voices wailing, praying, pleading in fear. And then the sound cut off, abruptly as though a door had closed to shut it out. At the same moment the ship appeared again.

It wasn't as though it had fallen over sideways, to be hidden by the rearing waves. It flickered into existence there, all outlined in green fire. There were figures crawling up from under hatches, green and glowing. One by one they slid down the deck into the water; and the first one pulled the second after it into the depths, and the second pulled the third, because they were chained together.

"It's a slave ship," roared Sejanus. Another and another and another went into the furious sea, pulled out of sight by the weight of their chains. John found his face was wet with tears. There was no way to get out to them, no way to stop what was unfolding.

"For the love of God!" screamed Mrs. Waverly. "*Please—*"

And then they were gone. The wreck blinked out again, between one heartbeat and the next. Green spume floated in the air around the rock. Another flash of lightning revealed nothing there, but wind gusted up from the beach and brought the melancholy chanting of voices.

John turned to Sejanus. "You seen it, didn't you? You *knew* it was there!"

Sejanus backed away, shaking his head. "It wasn't real. There's things in our skulls that get out, and make shadows to scare us. Old stories. Memories. *But they aren't real!*"

There was a high-pitched scream. Mr. Tudeley was staring and pointing far down the beach. They turned and saw the green figures making their way ashore, crawling from the glowing waves, rising awkwardly to their chained feet. They lurched and shuffled as they came. They were only black in the flashes of lightning. The thunder sounded like drums now, rolling steady.

Mr. Tudeley turned and fled for the shelter, clutching at his hat; Mrs. Waverly was already gone. John grabbed Sejanus by the arm.

"What do we do, damn you?"

Sejanus shook his hand off. "Build up the fire!" he shouted. "Turn your back and stop believing in them. They got no power to harm us!"

"If you say so," said John. He turned and hurried to the fire, that had been fanned by the relentless wind so that it had eaten through all the fuel they'd piled on it and was now low and blue, crawling over the bed of coals. Mr. Tudeley was crouched under the tree behind it, gulping down rum like water. Mrs. Waverly had crawled into the shelter and sat there huddled up, her eyes tight shut.

John threw down his crutch. He grabbed wood from their store and tossed it on, one log, another, two more, and sparks flew up against the black sky but no blaze caught. Craning his head back to follow the sparks' flight, John saw the clouds churning above the island, like a maelstrom in the air. He looked down helplessly at the blue flames and the memory came unbidden from childhood:

All Hallow's Eve, and he'd sat with his brothers and sisters around the fire, pushing hazelnuts in amongst the coals and raking them out when they'd popped. His dad and the uncles had sat on benches, passing the jug of cider back and forth, and his mum and the aunts came in from taking the cakes out of the oven in the yard. They weren't allowed to sing, lest the neighbors hear, but they'd made merry anyhow; and then his grandam had sat and told a

fearful story, all about a girl going out to weep on her lover's grave. They'd listened in silence. The fire had fallen low and blue, the warmth had gone out of the room as Grandam spoke. Then the wind had risen suddenly and the yard-door flown open with a bang. John had looked up and seen a man standing there, only for a moment. Aunt Ella had screamed and screamed, then, crying that it was her Charlie who'd been drowned at sea...

But here and now the sand hissed, the palm fronds rattled like shot in the warm wind, and the crawling fire writhed among the coals, pink and blue and yellow, all colors from the salt in the driftwood. The palm trees all around bent and swayed like dancers. Sejanus was beside him, pitching more wood on the fire, but nothing could get it to blaze up. Smoke began to rise from its center, spiraling up to meet the whirling cloud above, a looming darkness even the flashes of lightning could not pierce. In desperation, John grabbed up his crutch and shoved it in amongst the coals.

"How are we not supposed to be afeared of this, mate?" he shouted at Sejanus.

"It's just a storm!"

"But I seen—"

"Stop that!" Sejanus advanced on Mr. Tudeley, who was dipping and gulping from the rum barrel, dipping and gulping with his eyes closed. "You'll kill your damn self!"

He struck the coconut shell from Mr. Tudeley's hands. It went flying into the fire, and Mr. Tudeley seemed like to fly in after it. But as he started up with his eyes open, the rum sent the fire roaring high at last, an explosion of heat and light.

Mr. Tudeley staggered back. His hat blew off and landed in the fire.

There was an impact like thunder, but without sound. The wind stopped utterly.

Mr. Tudeley was jolted forward, as though someone had struck him across the shoulders. He regained his balance and lifted his head, slowly. Before this hour his eyes had been a rather watery blue: the eyes that regarded Sejanus now were black, rimmed in red.

"*Bandele*," he said, in a voice not his own.

Sejanus drew himself up, scowling. "No Bandele here," he said. "Bandele was a little shirttail slave boy. He watched his daddy shake that old rattle and offer up half his victuals, and pray till his throat cracked—all to an old piece of wood daubed up with paint. Old wood never answered him, never helped him, never did a damned thing but sit there!

"And I'm Sejanus Walker, for better or worse. I was born a slave, but I walked out of my master's house on my own. You never helped me and you never helped my daddy. Chah! I'm not obliged to you for shite, whatever you are, and I don't need you now!"

What had been Mr. Tudeley chuckled, a dry chuckle like a mild old man.

"Don't you vent your temper on me, son," it said. "I'm just the gatekeeper. You want a shouting match? There's some here will be pleased to take you on."

The red color in the eyes intensified, until they became balls of blood. The features writhed, the teeth drew back from the lips in wrath. The voice, when it came, boomed out a resonant bass.

"You ungrateful little cockroach! You think it's easy, fool, finding a way to make that passage across the ocean?

You think it's easy, coming to a land where there's already spirits, and they aren't willing to make room? You think we weren't weak as blocks of old wood, when we got across at last, with all the children scattered and frightened and forgetting us?

"*Damn* you! Haven't we walked beside you day and night, and come between you and harm a dozen times? Ha! You don't need us, Bandele? So you say! But *they* do!"

The figure thrust out a pointing finger. John turned his head to see what it pointed at, and promptly wished he hadn't; for the black wet dead stood in their ranks beyond the palisadoes, looking on melancholy. Some were naked and chained. Some were clothed in rags. Some were decently clad in shirts and trousers or gowns but just as dead, with grave-mould in their hair. One and all they held their arms out, in pitiful longing.

Sejanus glanced over his shoulder at them and froze. He couldn't look away. John must, though, and so he saw the figure dip up rum in its two hands and mouth it, and spray it out across the fire. Flame shot out and reflected in the eyes of the dead. They looked hopeful, reaching for the warmth; but it faded and was gone.

The figure sagged, twisted, seemed in pain. It spat out the rum, pursing its lips in distaste, wiping its mouth. It opened eyes white-pale as the moon and spoke in a woman's voice, infinitely reproachful.

"Oh, Bandele, how could you be so cruel? Look at them! Lost in a stranger's country. No rites said over them, no one to look after their souls. They're hungry. They're cold. They're lost. Some drowned in the wrecks, some were beaten to death, some were worked to death. Who's going to help these dead children, lost on this shore? Who's going to pull them up out of the water and set them free?"

Sejanus found his voice. "What do they want with me?" he said, very quiet.

The figure stood taller, worked its shoulders easily, spoke in the voice of a serene and magisterial male. "You know. You know in your bones. Your daddy was a weak man, but his blood was strong. Your mama was an ugly woman, but her blood was lovely. They came of mighty lines and you are their child, born *here*. Your power is here in this new place. You were marked for us from the moment you touched this earth."

"But I don't believe," said Sejanus hopelessly.

The figure grinned. "Oh, child, you *know*. You don't have to believe. You don't have to give us maize or peas or liquor. You don't even have to love us. But you will help those poor souls rest because you know you must."

"But how? How am I to help them?" shouted Sejanus.

The figure shrank, bent, and once again Mr. Tudeley could almost be discerned. The little chuckle came again, scornful. "Oh, *now* he wants our advice. Mr. Sejanus Walker, the high-and-mighty atheist. Serve you right if we closed our mouths again and let you figure it all out for yourself. You're a smart child; you could do it. But maybe we'll help, a little. You'll have to wait and see…"

Abruptly the presence, or presences, were gone. Mr. Tudeley dropped like a puppet whose strings had been cut, and lay motionless beside the fire. The silence broke; once again they heard the surf pounding on the beach, the distant rumble of thunder as the storm moved away to the north. A wind rustled the palm leaves and swept the smoke of the fire up in gusts, to the clearing sky where a few stars shone out.

Something moved, black against the stars. Something was fluttering down out of the night, turning over and over as it fell. It dropped at Sejanus's feet. Both he and John stared at it.

It was a man's hat, in the most elegant cut of the latest fashion, all black watered silk. It had a black rooster's tail for a cockade, held on with a silver pin in the shape of a cross. Sejanus bent and picked it up, cautiously. He began to swear, in a despairing kind of way.

John looked over at the palisadoes and saw the dead were gone. He looked back and met Sejanus's gaze.

"Now, I'll tell you where this came from," said Sejanus, turning the hat in his hands. "This was some Frenchman's, or Spanish lord's hat. That hurricane must have swept it off his head, from some ship out at sea. It just blew around in the upper air until it came down here. That's all."

"Right," said John. "You going to put it on?"

Sejanus looked at the hat with profound dislike. "No reason not to. It's just a hat. Stylish hat, too. Doesn't mean anything if I try it on."

He set it on his head. It fit; it even suited him. It made him look rakish and wise.

"Mr. James," said a calm voice near the ground. John nearly jumped out of his skin, and looked down to see Mrs. Waverly staring up at him from underneath the shelter. Her eyes were wide and terrified, for all the control she had over her tone. "I believe I should like it if you would be so kind as to sleep with me tonight."

So John lay down and slept with her, and that was all he did. He couldn't have got his prick up that night even if she'd been the queen of Sheba.

SIXTEEN:

A Surprise

MRS. WAVERLY WAS A little cold to him next morning. John would have thought she'd have made some comment about the ghosts and spirits that had come calling, but no indeed; only the fact that John hadn't been up for a jolly tumble seemed to weigh with her, this morning.

Mr. Tudeley also had no memory of the night past, it seemed. He lay like one dead by the fire until just after sunrise, when he scrambled up on his hands and knees and puked into the coals. The resultant blast of flame therefrom singed off his eyebrows. Afterward he sat in the shade and complained peevishly about the damned poor quality of the rum.

Nor did Sejanus seem to have any desire to mention his unwanted guests. He wore his new hat, however, when they walked back down from the camp to work on the pinnace.

John crawled into Mrs. Waverly's little boudoir of canvas that night, by way of apology, but she minced no words in explaining to him that she hadn't offered a standing invitation to her person by any means.

The pinnace took shape quickly. If it wasn't the most elegant craft ever built it was at least seaworthy, as they found when they floated the hull after it had been well tarred with some of the Dutchman's stores. They put in thwarts and stepped a little mast, made from one of the *Harmony's* spars, and rigged a jib sail. All that remained was to finish a bit of a half-deck at the stern, where cargo might be stored or Mrs. Waverly might retire in privacy.

In regard to which, the lady seemed to have thought better of her adamantine chastity somewhat, at least as far as what hands and lips might do; for she lured John away two nights running for a stroll along the beach at sunset. There she eloquently persuaded him of her lasting devotion and fond hope that he'd squire her around the Continent, after they should claim the four thousand pounds. So pleasantly she backed her words with deeds that John barely noticed the dead men the last tide had brought up to festoon the sand, though they were getting pretty disgraceful now.

"These are the last I could shake free," said Mr. Tudeley, struggling over the sand with a netful of coconuts. "Really, need we bring any more?"

"You'll want 'em if we get becalmed on our way," said John. "I make it two weeks to Leauchaud. Six coconuts per person per day, that's three hundred thirty-six coconuts."

"There'll be no room for *us* in the damned thing, then!"

"Ah." John laid a finger beside his nose. "We load 'em in the boat and tow it after us, see? Which will be handy to have anyhow in case the pinnace sinks."

"It won't sink," said Sejanus, loading in the little chest of navigational gear. "Have a little faith."

"Faith in what exactly?" said John, glowering after him. "That bit of high wind brought you your fancy hat?"

Sejanus shrugged. "I have all the faith I need, in myself. I don't plan on dying just yet. Too much to do."

"There's some palms in a grove the far side of that rock," said John to Mr. Tudeley. "Whyn't you go see what you can collect over there?" When Mr. Tudeley had gone tramping off with an empty net, muttering savagely, John turned back to Sejanus.

"What'll you do now, after you leave us off at Leauchaud?" he asked. "Sign on with the Brethren? Or set up shop as an obeah man?"

Sejanus raised an eyebrow. "No reason I can't do both, is there? The one's a good way to finance the other, seems to me. But I won't be serving the orishas. I'm no houngan; I have other things to do."

"You don't believe in 'em?" John stopped work and stared at him. "After what happened the other night?"

"Chah! Of course I believe in *them*. Not impressed. Didn't you hear 'em, all pushing and shoving to talk through one poor little old white man? They're weak; this isn't their country. But it's mine." Sejanus looked out on the Caribbean. "I'll have to imagine something new. Buy myself a fancy coat, maybe, to go with my hat, and a walking stick to impress folk. Deal a little in the old tricks. Good luck charms, poppets for barren women, fortunetelling, just to build a reputation, you see?

"Get a new religion going, then. Tell blacks: doesn't matter if your bones don't lie in Africa. You won't be cold and lonely in the dark here, once you die; somebody's going to look after you. You'll be dancing and drinking good rum, and eating sweet cake!

"And if I can make them believe it, truly believe it, then it'll be so. That's how religion works, friend."

Once upon a time John might have laughed at him, or told him he was a liar. But John thought back on the things he'd seen and done here, in the West Indies, since he'd escaped from the cane fields and gone on the account. On sober consideration, he just grunted and shook his head.

"Hope you get away with it, mate."

They worked on in silence a while, loading in gear and fastening it down. John retrieved the swivel gun from the salvage-pile and looked at it fondly. He had cleaned and scoured it out with sand, and greased it well with goat fat, and greased up the sack of one-pound balls too.

"Reckon we ought to mount it on the stern, just in case?" he said. Sejanus eyed him.

"You're precious fond of that gun, for a man who's going to quit the Brethren and become an honest bricklayer."

"Well, it handles prettily," said John. "And you never can tell what sort of bastards are going to come sailing up astern, can you?"

"Just like all those cutlasses you're stowing away will be useful opening coconuts," said Sejanus. "And the pistol and balls be useful for shooting seagulls, eh?"

"Old habits die hard," said John. Mr. Tudeley came trudging up.

"I have here thirty-six coconuts," he announced in a

martyred voice. "And I'm going to go recline in the shade and drink rum now, and if you attempt to stop me, sir, I shall run a cutlass through your damned liver."

"Peace, Wint," said Sejanus. "Don't see why we mayn't stop work for today, anyhow. We can finish up in the morning."

"I reckon so," said John. He heaved his sea chest in over the side of the pinnace and dusted his hands.

They went together up the trail they'd worn through the sea-grape, single file. John came over the crest of the ridge and looked down into the camp. He frowned in puzzlement. He looked out at the horizon. The others slammed into him, as into a wall.

"Damn you, sir!" said Mr. Tudeley. John ignored him and ran down the hill through the camp, which was in disarray, and jumped the palisadoes and kept going down to the beach, which was crossed with many pairs of footprints, and splashed out into the surf to gaze after the black sloop, which was halfway to the horizon.

SEVENTEEN:

Pursuit

"**B**LEEDING JESUS, SHE BEEN** kidnapped," John muttered. He backed out of the surf, thinking all the while of his share of the four thousand pounds, and feeling mean and small to be so mercenary, but there it was. He turned to the others. "We have to go after her!"

"Ha! I expect the lady will vigorously defend herself," said Mr. Tudeley, but on seeing John's face, Sejanus grabbed him and turned him around.

"Don't argue, Wint. A gentleman always helps a lady in distress, eh? Come on!"

They ran back up and over the island. By the time they got to the pinnace John was in such a rage that he seized its stern and launched it himself, shoving it down the shingle beach as though it was a toy boat. The others splashed through the shallows and vaulted in over the gunwales as he was setting the sail.

"You take the tiller," John told Sejanus. "And *you* can

sit down and keep your bloody mouth shut if you ain't got anything helpful to say!"

"Quite," said Mr. Tudeley. "I don't suppose we remembered the rum?"

John turned from him, snarling. For the next few minutes he was very busy handling the sail, but at last they came around the end of the island and spotted the black sloop, now nearly hull-down on the horizon.

John ranted and swore, until they picked up a favorable breeze and the pinnace shot forward, racing over the swells. The water broke fair and white on the prow, whispered along the hull and creamed out into a cleft wake. He thought of Mrs. Waverly's white thighs, at least her thighs as he'd imagined them, and how he might never see them in the flesh now. He thought of two thousand pounds in gold, and how Mrs. Waverly was the only person with any idea where Tom had hidden it, and how there'd be no way to recover the loot should anything untoward happen to her.

The pinnace proved more than seaworthy; she was swift. They arrowed along after the sloop, keeping her in sight, and steadily over the hours crept up on her.

"Who do you suppose they are?" said Mr. Tudeley, at last.

"Kidnappers, who d'you think?" John growled. He had been straining to make out details on the craft, and could see no flag.

"They don't seem in much of a hurry to run away from us," said Sejanus, shading his eyes with his hand. "Not much sail set. Good thing, too; she looks as though she could cut through the water pretty fast, if she had a mind to."

"She does indeed," said Mr. Tudeley. "I expect they don't know we're after them."

"That would be handy," said Sejanus.

Mr. Tudeley lifted the flap of a canvas bundle, and looked down at the cutlasses John had stowed there that afternoon. "Upon my word, Mr. James, you've armed us well. Just the sort of things one would need for a daring rescue."

"Didn't know I'd need 'em though, did I?" said John, squinting over his shoulder at the low red sun. "Damn! It'll be night soon."

Mr. Tudeley looked thoughtfully after the sloop. "I wonder how many fellows are on board?"

"Wouldn't take many to carry off one woman," said John. "The bastards!"

"They probably came ashore for to get water," said Sejanus, rubbing his chin. "Funny we didn't hear any screaming for help, or anything."

"Isn't it?" Mr. Tudeley gave him a significant look. "Perhaps they weren't pirates. Perhaps it's a trading vessel."

"With cargo on board? Hmm."

"Rum, perhaps." Mr. Tudeley licked his lips. "I wonder how well they're armed?"

"Shame we had to leave the boat behind," said Sejanus. "Hope we don't spring a leak. I'll bet that sloop doesn't leak. It looks fine and seaworthy."

"So it does," said Mr. Tudeley.

"What are you lot babbling about?" demanded John in exasperation.

"Not much," said Sejanus, poking the sack of one-pound balls. "Look behind you, Wint. I think you're leaning on a powder keg, aren't you?"

"I am indeed," said Mr. Tudeley. "And here's a coil of slow-match. I wonder if one might start a little blaze in, say, a coconut shell like this one? If one packed in a bit of tinder. Here are wood chips aplenty, under the thwarts. They'd smolder nicely."

"Flint and steel in the navigation box."

"Is there? There is! That's useful."

"They're lighting her stern lanterns!" announced John. "That's something anyhow. We won't lose 'em in the dark!"

"Oh, good." Mr. Tudeley took out a clasp-knife and began methodically shaving bits off the gunwale, tucking the long dry curls into his coconut shell.

"Shame we haven't got all those coconuts you gathered, Wint," said Sejanus. He looked over his shoulder, where the island had receded to a mere irregularity on the horizon, black against the sunset. "Here we are at sea with almost no provisions. We're going to be powerfully thirsty soon."

"I fear so," said Mr. Tudeley. He looked sidelong at Sejanus. "Life is a rather grim matter of survival, after all. One must do what one must."

"That's a fact for certain," Sejanus drawled. "*Ad victorem spolias.*"

"I'd no idea you were so well educated, sir. How pleasant. 'To the victors go the spoils!' Words to live by, indeed." Mr. Tudeley reached into the instrument chest for flint and steel, and set about making a few coals to smolder in his coconut shell.

They kept the sloop in sight through the night hours, John watching her stern lanterns all the while in agony of mind. Mrs. Waverly had not seemed like the sort of woman to kill herself over a bit of violation, but his imagination

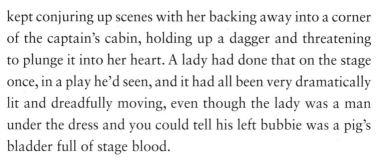

kept conjuring up scenes with her backing away into a corner of the captain's cabin, holding up a dagger and threatening to plunge it into her heart. A lady had done that on the stage once, in a play he'd seen, and it had all been very dramatically lit and dreadfully moving, even though the lady was a man under the dress and you could tell his left bubbie was a pig's bladder full of stage blood.

And perhaps John nodded off where he sat once or twice, because the twin beaming stern lanterns seemed to be shining out from Mrs. Waverly's shift, and she hoisted up her shift and revealed her bubbies shining like lamps, bright and hard and hot, and she was begging of him to cool them down, so badly had she sunburned on that island...

They were getting bigger, and bigger. He hadn't thought a woman's bubbies ever got that big. They were like two suns now. "Oh, Mr. James," she was whimpering, "Do something! Please! I'm ever so hot!"

They were so hot they were setting fire to her shift. He could smell the burning. It smelled like saltpeter...

He realized with a start that the sloop's stern lanterns were very near now, and Mr. Tudeley had just lit a length of slow match and was saying, in a complacent tone: "There! Quite serviceable, I think. Shall you carry the pistol, or shall I?"

John rubbed his eyes and looked around. Dawn was coming up pink in the east. The sloop was no more than a half-mile off now. Mr. Tudeley had unwrapped the cutlasses and was sorting through them, weighing each in his hand for balance.

"*Very* nice," he said, taking an experimental swipe at the air with one. "And I suppose one just lays about one as though one were wielding a meat cleaver."

"That's the way," said Sejanus.

"I must endeavor not to lose my other ear this time. What ho, Mr. James! A good morning to you. She's a fair ship, is she not?"

John peered across at the sloop, where it cruised there backlit by the dawn. Low and rakish, with elegant lines, it was still just idling along. The silhouetted helmsman wasn't even bothering to look behind him.

John clenched his fists, feeling the return of his anger. How many might be aboard? Five men? Six? Had they all had their way with Mrs. Waverly? Had she, perhaps in fear of her life, told them about the four thousand pounds? Were they even now on their way to Leauchaud?

He reached around and grabbed up the swivel gun, and loaded it with a pair of one-pound balls. "Where's the damned powder?"

"Ready," said Mr. Tudeley, handing him the powder horn. "Match?"

"Aye." John took the length of slow-match and clamped it between his teeth while he filled the touch-hole and stuck a couple of extra balls in his coat pocket.

"I don't think we want to give them a one-pound broadside," Sejanus cautioned. John shook his head, glaring. They came alongside the sloop, making out her name at last: *Le Rossignol*. The helmsman saw them now, and filled his lungs to cry the alarm. John stood up on a thwart and aimed at him with the swivel gun, touching fire to powder with the match in his teeth.

"You idiot—" began Sejanus.

Boom! The helmsman was blown clear overboard, and John himself nearly pitched backward out of the pinnace.

Sejanus and Mr. Tudeley swarmed up over the sloop's rail as the sun rose, brandishing weapons. When John had caught his balance and reloaded he followed them.

Sleepy men came boiling up on deck, to face a terrible sight: a giant hoisting a cannon in his arms to aim it at them, and to one side a grinning black devil with a pair of cutlasses and a horde of shadows at his shoulder, and to the other side a ragged creature in the nadir of his fall from grace—bloodlust in his eye, snarling gap-toothed as he swung his blade, his broken spectacles glinting in the golden light of the sun.

There followed a brief but quite bloody fray. One of the crew threw down his weapon and fell to his knees. Three unwisely decided to fight, and died there on the deck, one half-beheaded and shot by Mr. Tudeley and another run through by Sejanus, with the third smashed down by John's fist. Last of all a handsome man came rushing up shirtless from the great cabin, a slender elegant-looking fellow with a little downy mustache of the sort ladies fancy on a man. John ground his teeth. He took aim with the swivel gun and blew the captain clear to Hell.

Still clutching the smoking swivel gun, John shouldered his way down into the great cabin. "Ma'am!" he roared. "Ma'am! Are y'in here?"

"I told you, you filthy brigand, I shall never yield my honor!" cried a voice from the stern gallery head.

"It's me, ma'am! John James! We've rescued you!"

"Oh!" cried Mrs. Waverly, flinging the cabinet door wide. "Oh, Mr. James, how heroic!"

She wore her nightdress, a lace one with ribbons; he'd seen it in her trunk when he'd opened it, that one time. There wasn't a bruise or any other mark on her, that he could see. She flung her arms around his neck. He smelled perfume as she kissed him.

"Oh, Mr. James! I have been beside myself with fear! However did you find me? I reclined to rest in the heat of the day—I think I must have fallen asleep—and when next I opened my eyes, there were the most dreadful grinning blackguards standing over me! Why I wasn't ravished on the spot I cannot imagine, unless that they intended their chief should dishonor me himself.

"They carried me off, along with my effects. Yet I was able to break free, dear Mr. James, and barricade myself in that closet. What might have happened had you not effected your timely rescue, I shudder to think!"

"Well, it don't signify now," said John, noting that her hair had been neatly brushed, and wondering whether he hadn't just murdered three innocent men. "We're off the island and back on our way to Leauchaud. No harm done, eh?"

"None, I faithfully promise you," said Mrs. Waverly, melting against him. He helped himself to another kiss. He would have helped himself to more but her eyelids fluttered, and she passed the back of her hand across her brow. "Oh, dear—I feel faint—oh, to consider what I so narrowly escaped!"

"Maybe you ought to have a lie down then," said John, resignedly helping her to the captain's bed, which was in a certain state of disarray. He went out to see that her lover's blood was sluiced off the deck before she should come out and have to notice it.

Mr. Tudeley and Sejanus were already pitching bodies over as he came up the companionway, aided by the one man who had surrendered.

"John, this is Portuguese Fausto," said Sejanus. "He's given us to understand he was only hired on as a cook two weeks ago, and the crew treated him badly so he doesn't hold it against us that we had to kill them. He says he doesn't see how you could have done any different, what with them running off with your wife and all." Portuguese Fausto nodded in vehement agreement.

"And the hold contains several crates of china porcelain and twenty-five kegs of Spanish brandy," said Mr. Tudeley in satisfaction. "Which will, I suspect, fetch us a goodly price in Tortuga. Such of it as is not consumed on the journey, of course."

"Would he cook us some breakfast?" said John.

"Sim, senhor!" Portuguese Fausto's face brightened. "Breakfast, straightaway!"

"I'll just go watch, to see he doesn't put too much salt in anything," said Sejanus, drawing his cutlass and following the cook below hatches. John and Mr. Tudeley rigged a tow line to the pinnace, struck her sail, and let out a little more of *Le Rossignol's* canvas. John sagged into the helmsman's seat, bone-tired suddenly, and took the tiller.

Mr. Tudeley, by comparison, strutted up and down the deck admiring their new vessel.

"All that exertion, and yet, do you know, I feel as nimble as a boy?" he remarked. "Only think of it, sir! I have just killed a man; I have just taken a prize by main force, and am about to enjoy my ill-gotten gains; I'd be hanged for this in any court you care to name, and damned for a villain of deepest dye. Yet, sir, yet, my heart is as light as thistledown! How full of promise is this bright morning! Is it not extraordinary?"

"*'You see the world turn'd upside down,'*" quoted John dully.

"So it has," said Mr. Tudeley, and hummed a few bars of the old song. "Ah, well!"

EIGHTEEN:

Hot Water

THEY WERE NINE DAYS out from Leauchaud, as it happened, which was plenty of time to wash and shave and put on good clothes. Sejanus, who had no sea-chest, took possession of the dead captain's, and found that most of the fine garments fit him. So they were quite a civilized-looking crew that sailed into Maingauche Harbor, except for Mr. Tudeley, whose appearance had been rendered permanently disreputable.

"Much I care," he said cheerily, over his breakfast brandy. "I've gone on the account! I should think a fearsome countenance suits a pirate."

"It don't hurt," John admitted.

"You ought to join us," said Sejanus, tilting his hat back. "We need a good crew, Wint and me. It'll be profitable, I can promise you." But John shook his head.

"I've pushed my luck far enough. I'm done with the Brethren. Always fancied dying in my bed."

"You'll certainly die in *her* bed," said Mr. Tudeley

with a snigger, glancing in the direction of the great cabin. Mrs. Waverly was in there, singing serenely as she combed out her hair.

"Oh, har har har," said John. "I should hope so. I reckon we'll get married after all."

"Good luck," said Sejanus. "But it's been known to happen, now and again, that a woman changes her mind. We'll lie up here a few days. Take on some supplies, see can we sign on a few crewmen. You need a berth after all, you just come by and see us."

So John went ashore at Leauchaud, carrying both his sea chest and Mrs. Waverly's trunk, just as he'd started out the journey. Mrs. Waverly walked beside him, closely eyeing the place.

"Oh, it's very like Bath," she said.

"Is it?" John, who had never been out of London in all his days before being transported, looked up curiously. The whole place was built of cream-colored stone, from the eating-houses and taverns along the seafront to a few grand-looking buildings farther back. The green jungle came down behind.

"Very like," Mrs. Waverly repeated. "Perhaps we ought to find lodging first. You have still a little money left, have you not?"

Which John had, his three pounds from sacking the *Santa Ysabel* with the last pitiful scraps of his loot from the Panama expedition. Grumbling rather, he bespoke them a room at the Dancing Master, and was grateful to set down the trunks and take a glass of rum whist the room was got ready. Mrs. Waverly introduced herself to a quite respectable-looking sugar merchant and his wife and wife's sister, who were there to take the waters. She chatted away with them gaily, quite charming the merchant, if the ladies not so much, and from them learned a great deal. At last the landlord came back down and told them their room was ready.

"One bed, eh?" John observed, when they had got upstairs.

"Yes," said Mrs. Waverly. "We can afford better once we've recovered some of the money."

"Fair enough," said John, looking at her bubbies with regret. "Well, what do we do now? Borrow a shovel from the landlord, and go digging?"

"No," said Mrs. Waverly, looking a little pained at his simplicity. "You shall have a bath, Mr. James."

She explained no more until they were walking in the portico under the great iron sign reading SHILLITOE'S BATHS, watching well-to-do folk wander in and out of the pump room clutching little cups of water.

"Tom's instructions were to go into the baths reserved for gentlemen," said Mrs. Waverly. "Which you shall do, and seek out a third alcove on the left hand side. He said that if you go to the midmost ring set in the wall, and wait until you are alone, you may then dive down to the step below. He said there is a stone loose there; he said that if you pulled it out and reached into the hollow space behind, you should find the money."

"He said that, did he?" said John, irritated, for he now saw clearly enough why she had needed his help. She gave a little apologetic shrug.

"Poor Tom. He was a close man, as no doubt you came
to know. I do not think it was in his nature to trust anyone.
Shall we go in? I quite envy you. After so long on that island
and aboard ship, I positively long for a lovely bathe."

"How am I to carry the money out with me? Folk
will notice."

"So they should, if you brought it all out with you at
once! But of course we shan't do that, dear Mr. James."
She squeezed his arm. "I have been revolving in my mind
how Tom managed it. I think it likeliest he stayed a few days
and smuggled in the sealed bags two and three at a time,
perhaps. And so we must remove them in the same wise,
you see?"

"I reckon so," said John, wondering how big a hole Tom
had been able to make in the stone wall of a bath, and how
nasty might be the flooded place behind it. Mrs. Waverly
must have seen his doubts in his face, for she kissed him and
said gaily:

"Think how much pleasanter this shall be than diving
on the wrecks. It should be a most importunate shark that
swum ashore and came creeping about bathhouses!"

So they went into the pump room. Here Mrs. Waverly
found an impressive-looking gentleman in a white plumed hat
who was the Bath Constable. She gave him a song and dance
about her dear husband requiring the waters for his health,
and wanting to know to whom he might apply to bathe?

Whereupon the Bath Constable smiled broadly, and
paid Mrs. Waverly many compliments, and recommended to
her many excellent establishments on the island for millinery,
shoes and the like, as well as notable local wonders worth
renting a coach to see. He discoursed a little on the state

of modern medicine and quackery nostrums one ought to avoid, and listed the multitude of complaints and diseases completely cured by resort to Shillitoe's Baths, which were after all compounded by no less an eminent apothecary than Almighty God Himself.

But the end was, John had to pay out the very last of his Panama silver to be led into an antechamber where a couple of mournful-looking youths in white canvas clothes disrobed him, and handed his clothes out the door to Mrs. Waverly. They then dressed him in loose trousers and a sort of shift of canvas, so immense John might have made a pretty commodious tent out of it. They then led him through another door and, taking his arms, walked him down some steps into the Gentlemen's Baths.

"I can wash myself, mate," said John, shaking them off.

"You're a h'invalid, ain't you?" protested one of the youths.

"Do I look like a fucking invalid to you?" said John, and they admitted he didn't, and retired posthaste back up the stairs.

He gazed around. The Gentlemen's Baths looked like a church with all the pews taken out, and flooded, and having no glass in the high windows. He was in a big domed room, from which an aisle led with alcoves opening off it to right and left. All around the edges, set halfway up the walls, were bronze rings. Here and there was a miserable-looking old gent in a canvas shift, holding on to a ring for dear life, while attendants stood by watching lest he drown. The whole place stank like a fart.

Third alcove, left hand side, John thought to himself, and waded down into the pool. At once the trapped air in his clothes ballooned up, buoying him, and before he had taken more than a few awkward steps across the room, the water down by his feet became scalding hot. He danced, back, swearing. An attempt to launch himself forward and swim across nearly got him drowned as well as boiled, for the clothes kept hindering his arms and legs. He fetched up against the wall, clutching for one of the bronze rings, and hauled himself up on a sort of shelf that projected below the waterline.

"D'you need assistance, sir?" called one of the attendants, grinning.

"No, damn you," said John, wiping his face. He worked out that the shelf was continuous around the room and down the aisle, so he proceeded to follow it, wading and bobbling from ring to ring, out of the main chamber and so along the wall.

He wondered how Tom had ever managed this while carrying gold, even small sealed bags of five-guinea pieces. He had a sudden powerful memory of Tom, with his little pointed beard and his knowing smirk. Tom indeed; tomcat cavalier fallen on hard times, living by his wits. He'd been clever enough to hide a prince's ransom in here, safe against Spanish intriguers or English cutthroats. Or his own dear lady love...

It hadn't escaped John that Mrs. Waverly had firm custody of his clothes. Not that he would be able to make off with the loot in any case; the windows were too high and well barred, the canvas garments impossible to run in. Smuggling the stuff out, at least, ought to be easy enough; John might have stowed a barrel under his shift, with room for a couple of kegs.

He made his way past the first two alcoves on the left and into the third, which was deserted, perhaps because there was a nasty-looking slime the color of orange peel growing in a wide patch on the wall.

...Go to the midmost ring...

Balancing on the shelf there, he took a deep breath and ducked under the water, feeling with his fingers for a loose stone. Almost at once, before he could discern anything there, the air-bubble of his shift pulled him back up again. He tried a second and third time before standing up on the shelf and stripping off the shift, muttering to himself as he hung it through the ring. Then he took a deep breath and dove down.

In the simmering gloom, peering through the vaguely rust-tinted water, John saw that he might have crouched there groping about forever without finding the loose stone; it wasn't above the shelf but under it, only just visible for the dark rectangle where the mortar had been chipped away. How long had *that* taken Tom?

John caught hold of the edges of the stone and rocked it to and fro and so out by degrees, though the edges bit into his fingertips and he had to come up for air again before he pulled it away. Panting, he laid it on the shelf and reached into the hole.

Almost at once his fingers struck solid stone. He grunted in pain and withdrew his hand; he'd fair skinned his knuckles. More cautiously, he reached in and felt about. He encountered only the flat sides of the hole. It was big enough to accommodate the stone that had occupied it, and nothing else.

No...his palm encountered something. Smallish. Flat.

He drew it out and surfaced, gasping, to peer at it. A single coin? Not even that. It was a brass slug, engraved with the number 5.

Something kept him from flinging it across the alcove into the boiling water, to be retrieved by anyone who cared to get scalded. John turned it over. Something else was engraved on the back.

Ye Three Tunns

He knew the Three Tunns. It was a tavern in Port Royal. It had a livery stable in back, on an alley off Thames Street, where things might be left until called for. He'd never owned anything to store there, but he'd diced once with a fellow who'd laid down a token like this as surety, claiming that John might have the chest of pewter plate it would redeem. John had lost the throw so it hadn't mattered.

Of course Tom hadn't dragged a chest of gold all the way to Leauchaud. He'd cached it at the Three Tunns and come here to hide the token, well away from Mrs. Waverly's quick fingers. Then he'd gone on, to Panama and his unexpected death.

John laughed quietly. It might have been the echoes, but he almost fancied he heard Tom's wry laughter too.

He put the token in his mouth, having no pockets, and put on the shift once more, and went splashing back out to the main chamber. When he emerged into the dressing-room, he found Mrs. Waverly sitting there chatting freely with the attendants. She stood quickly on seeing him.

"Well, husband dear! Has the water done you good, as we'd hoped?"

John spat the token into his hand. "Yes, thank'ee."

"Afford us some privacy, do," said Mrs. Waverly to the attendants. They elbowed one another and sidled out, snickering.

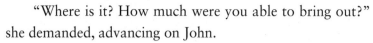
"Where is it? How much were you able to bring out?" she demanded, advancing on John.

"All of it," said John, and showed her the token. She stared at it a long moment, going quite pale under her fresh paint.

"Why, that bastard," she said.

NINETEEN:

The Inn in Thames Street

THEY QUARRELED ALL THE way back to the Dancing Master, and Tom Blackstone was called a few more choice names When they got to the tavern John went upstairs to get their trunks. Mrs. Waverly did her utmost to charm the landlord into refunding what they'd paid him for the privilege of giving their trunks a view of the harbor for three hours. He was disinclined to oblige on the matter, however. John got to watch Mrs. Waverly undergo a surprising transformation, with the veins in her neck standing out as she screamed a few epithets he hadn't heard since the last time he'd walked through the fish stalls of Billingsgate.

So they went penniless back to the waterfront, and were greatly relieved to see *Le Rossignol* drawn up to the quay. Sejanus was directing the loading-on of fresh water kegs and victuals, by Portuguese Fausto and two new crewmen, both blacks. He looked up at John and Mrs. Waverly, managing not to grin. "Afternoon," was all he said.

"Mr. Walker, we would be obliged to you for passage back to Port Royal," said Mrs. Waverly, rather short.

"Of course, ma'am," he replied, tipping his hat. She came up the gangplank and made straight for the great cabin without another word. John followed her with the trunks. Sejanus raised his eyebrows at him.

"Seems her late husband cut her out of the will," said John.

They skirted the edges of a storm, but otherwise had plain sailing back to Jamaica. Mr. Tudeley hung off the stern of the sloop and painted over the name *Le Rossignol*, renaming her *Revenge*, though John told him just about every other pirate vessel seemed to be named that nowadays. Then Mr. Tudeley said perhaps she ought to be *Tudeley's Revenge*, but Sejanus pointed out that simple *Revenge* was more nondescript and, given that they were about to engage in a life of crime, less easy to trace therefore. So *Revenge* she remained.

On a bright morning they dropped anchor just north of King's Wharf. John lowered his sea-chest and Mrs. Waverly's trunk into the pinnace, with a pair of oars.

"We'll be here a day or two," remarked Sejanus casually, leaning on the rail as John handed Mrs. Waverly down into the pinnace. "See can we get a good price for the china. We'll be off to Tortuga after that, with what's left of the brandy. Either sell it or trade it for a privateering commission. Sure you're not interested?"

"Steady sure, mate," said John.

Sejanus nodded to him. "Then good luck to you."

It was a long hot tramp down Thames Street in the morning heat, especially with a pair of trunks to carry. Mrs. Waverly stalked ahead of him, grimly purposeful, watching the signs. John, looking around, thought they might well have been dropped back in time to the morning they had set out. Nothing seemed to have changed much: same sticky salt mist lying over the town, same brilliant reflections of light and water on walls. He could feel a headache beginning in the back of his skull, from the glare.

He spotted the alleyway before Mrs. Waverly did and rushed ahead, shouldering his way through under the brick arch. She scuttled after him. The liveryman, lounging back on a bale of cotton, looked up in surprise as the pair of them reached his counter at once.

"We're redeeming something," said John, sliding the brass token across the counter. The liveryman took his red clay pipe from his mouth and leaned down to peer at the token.

"Five," he pronounced. "Indeed! I thought it was lost. Reverend Blackstone got his church built at last, hey?"

John blinked at him. "Aye. He did."

"I'll fetch it straight. Just bide, there; it's at the back." He walked away into the depths of the shed and they waited impatiently.

"*Reverend* Blackstone?" said John, sotto voce.

"I have no idea," said Mrs. Waverly, tapping her foot.

After a long while the liveryman came backing up to the counter, dragging a great chest after him.

"Here," he grunted, straightening up. "Whew! I've kept it the best part of a year...I make that two pounds ten in fees, sir and ma'am."

Mrs. Waverly gave him a brilliant smile. "You see we have just stepped ashore. Now, I will tell you what: I shall leave mine own trunk here as surety, while we just step next door and bespeak lodging. John, give the good man my trunk. And he shall give us the good Reverend's box."

The liveryman made a face, but John had already thumped Mrs. Waverly's trunk down on the counter, which was a plank across two barrels. The liveryman shoved the other trunk through beneath the counter and John hoisted it up, staggering a little at the weight.

They stepped across the alley into a place called the Feathers, quiet and empty at that hour of the morning. "Here!" said Mrs. Waverly, leading John to a dark corner of the common room. He set the chest down with a crash. Mrs. Waverly bent to unfasten the straps that closed it. Her hands were trembling. She threw back the lid.

"Bugger," said John in surprise. Within, neatly packed, were dozens of worn old copies of the *Book of Common Prayer.*

"No," said Mrs. Waverly. "No, no, no. Oh, you worthless son of a mongrel bitch." She raked the prayerbooks out. They spilled over on the floor until her nails grated across iron. She shoved more of the books out of the way to reveal the top of an ironbound box, and burst into tears. "Oh, Tom, forgive me!" she said.

Reaching into her bodice, she drew forth a key and cleared away enough prayerbooks to get at the lock. A moment and they had it open, to look upon a number of lumpy little waxed-canvas bags, each one sealed with the stamp of the House of Simmern.

John leaned down with his clasp-knife and slit one bag open. There, at last, he glimpsed bright gold. He tore with his fingers and they came sliding out, lovely five-guinea pieces. He grabbed a handful and stood, savoring the moment.

The landlord walked into the room then, wiping his hands on his apron and looking at them inquiringly.

"Your best room, my good sir," said Mrs. Waverly, blotting away her tears. "And your very best breakfast served up, and four bottles of your best rum."

They drank to Tom's memory, and dined on salt cod and maize cakes, with a pot of sweet chocolate. Before the end of the meal, Mrs. Waverly was sitting on John's lap, feeding him morsels from her fingertips. By the time they'd cleared the cloth, she had unlaced her bodice and was opening his breeches. John, nothing loth, carried her off to the bed, though he half expected she would go all faint on him again or exclaim that she had a headache.

To his amazement, she stripped off her clothes eagerly, and moreover helped him disrobe. She sprang onto the counterpane lithe as a tigress, and John followed rather more clumsily. What followed next was better than all his dreams.

They did not set foot to the floor all the rest of the day, save to go back to the dining table for the other bottles of rum. When they weren't fornicating madly they lay there passing the bottle back and forth, and Mrs. Waverly told

John all about the places they might go now, Paris or Rome or Amsterdam or Charleston.

Anywhere there was glittering Society, she explained, there were well-to-do folk who occasionally required certain services performed: indiscreet letters recovered, information gathered about the daily activities of junior princes or archdukes, the placing of well-born bastard children with suitably distant foster parents. These services paid quite well, apparently. Mrs. Waverly felt that a man of John's strength and imposing appearance would do very well at her side.

She told him much more, but by that time John had taken a great deal of rum on board and wasn't able to follow her words any too well. The last thing he remembered clearly was her telling him all about the fun to be had in Versailles at this time of year. Then she had rolled over, and invited him to do something he'd never done before. He wished afterward he could remember what it had been.

John woke alone, sick and groggy and near blind. The gray light of dawn was creeping in shamefaced, slow as though it was catching and tearing itself on all the masts and spars in the harbor.

He lay there a moment, trying to recollect where he was. When the memory came back, he rolled over and looked for Mrs. Waverly, but did not see her.

John fell out of bed and stared around the room. He saw his clothes, neatly folded on a chair, and his sea chest. The breakfast dishes were gone, and so were the empty rum bottles, but there was something white on the table. Moving unsteadily, he made his way to the table and peered down. He saw a piece of paper with writing on it.

Dearest John, I gave you my all, therefore I am taking your half.

He read it over three times, stupefied, before he caught the meaning. He looked around the room and saw that the big trunk was gone, along with its contents. She hadn't even left him a copy of the *Book of Common Prayer*.

John hadn't the strength to curse. Moving cautiously, lest his head fall off and shatter, he pulled on his clothes. He reflected that he was slightly better off than if he'd gone out drinking with Hairy Mary from the Turtle Crawl; she'd have taken his raiment and his sea chest too.

He went to the window and looked out. He could see five ships on the horizon, three of them already far out to sea, and Mrs. Waverly might be on any of them. As he stood there, running over the events of the past months in his mind, he remembered the four pearls he'd got when he'd looted the *Santa Ysabel's* great cabin. He'd kept them in their twist of paper, like peas in a pod, tucked in his spare shirt.

Opening his sea chest, John looked down at his clothes, that Mrs. Waverly had laundered and neatly folded. He rummaged through them. Lying atop the crossed arms of his spare shirt he found the twist of paper. On it she had written: *Pray excuse my little frailty.*

He sighed.

Walking along in the gloom before sunrise, John spotted the *Revenge* moored at the common landing by King's Wharf. Men were offloading boxes of china, silently and swiftly, and

Sejanus and Mr. Tudeley stood in quiet conversation with a merchant. Money exchanged hands. The china was trundled away on a cart. Sejanus and Mr. Tudeley were turning to go back on board when they spotted John.

Clearly, they had been ashore with money to spend. Sejanus had a fine black coat of watered silk to match his hat, and a silver-topped ebony walking stick. Mr. Tudeley had gotten a fearsome new tattoo on his chest, of a grinning skull above crossed bones. It was still bleeding slightly. To their credit, neither of them laughed as they watched John come slinking up with his sea chest on his shoulder.

"The lady changed her mind about marrying, did she?" said Mr. Tudeley. "I thought as much. Not really a suitable girl, old fellow."

"We're about to sail," said Sejanus. "Coming aboard?"

"It's only for a cruise or two," said John. "Just until I make enough of a pile to set myself up in a shop."

"To be sure," said Sejanus, with a straight face.

They went aboard the *Revenge*. Before the sun rose she was under sail, well past Deadman's Cay, bound for Tortuga.